FIRETONGUE

CHRONICLES OF THE CHOSEN

CASSANDRA BOYSON

KINGDOM HOUSE PRESS

Dedicated to HS,
for always rescuing me from the pit full of mud and mire
—

And in honor of the housewife who brandished a tent peg

CONTENTS

CHAPTER I

"HS, ARE YOU COMING?" Jaela whispered into the darkness. Flame wafted from her lips, illuminating the interior of the hollow tree. It was because of her malady that many called her daemonkind. Her mother, however, insisted she was chosen. Whatever the cause of her condition—blessing or curse—she coveted normalcy, to possess the ability to speak the tongue of her people, to communicate coherently with someone other than the one to whom she now called.

"I am here," her longtime friend echoed from the tops of the hollow.

"Took you long enough," she murmured with a satisfied sigh that made her flames spark.

Not since she was a small child had she uttered the language of her tribe. This was not of her volition. To her mind, she spoke plainly. What manifested in its place was a mysterious idiom.

Her mother claimed it was the tongues of angels. A very few questioned whether it was the dialect of "the ancients." Most believed her either born with a strain of daemon blood (likely her mother's side) or baffled of mind.

Whatever the true cause, she was branded a "wild thing." This was what the elders of the clan whispered when she responded to the peculiar impulses that sometimes accompanied her strange speech. There were times when she acted out bizarrely. The elders and leaders had no patience for someone of her idiosyncrasies. What could she contribute if she could not be depended upon?

But she was the child of Krin, her revered father. He had died what was deemed an honorable death. No matter their personal feeling toward Jaela and her mother, it was by the tribe's creed that they were required to treat the mother and daughter with "the honors"—seeing them fed, sheltered and clothed. Jaela could not be cast out, no matter who believed it justified.

The village's trouble with them was originally derived from the fact that her mother was not born of the archetypal forest clans. Evangeline had been of the River's Way, a community that had once dwelled beside the River Lifespring. This was before the Tribe of Deerskin, with whom they now lived, had eliminated her kind. Owing to her unparalleled beauty, she was the only survivor.

The River Lifespring was alleged to have cleansed the river people of their iniquities and even cured maladies. The vegetation that sprang up beside it had produced fruit of mystic quality. The river even decelerated the rate of aging for its shoreline inhabitants, causing them to live often hundreds of years beyond the standard, as well as fostering beauty that flourished with age.

Though a peaceable folk, those of the River's Way had endured for centuries. This was the chief reason that many had coveted the river's power. None had managed to conquer its people until the Tribe of Deerskin achieved it in a matter of days. It was whispered that the leader of the river people had turned over the key to their defenses in exchange for a compulsory marriage with Evangeline upon their victory. Therefore, the blood of the innocents had run into the river's current, unpredictably annulling its astounding properties. Though much had been sacrificed, Deerskin had gained nothing. As revenge, the leader of the River's Way had been slain. Evangeline was taken as a bride by Warrior Krin, the leader of the assault. Jaela was the product of these happenings.

"What have you to relate today?" Jaela asked her mystifying friend as he drifted down as a shimmering mist. Often, he arrived with news, an encouraging sentiment or whispered clues pertaining to her future, which he always insisted was good. Most days, she doubted it. Life appeared to her as if it would always be aimless and lonely.

As his form took shape beside her, his face, arms and torso were of shining bronze while his bottom portion was pure flame in place of legs. To be certain, he was a bizarre personage. But he claimed to be the very spirit-essence of the Great One himself. According to her mother, the Great One was what the tribes referred to as the Creator—the originator of the universe. Though most acknowledged the Creator's existence, they did not know him as had the river people once upon a time.

Seating himself comfortably beside Jaela, he answered, "I suggest you prepare your mother for your departure."

Her eyes shot to his face. His voice, though often playful, was solemn. She did not know what to make of such a statement. "My... *departure?*" Her throat went dry. She stole a moment to clear it before, "Am I going to... pass on?"

It did not sound so bad, truth be told. But she was all her mother had. Evangeline would be alone in the world. Moreover, the woman was typically sickly. Who would care for her?

"Nay," he answered gently. "You are to travel. I have a journey prepared for you... should you accept."

Jaela's eyes sought the dark membrane of the tree. She could not meet his gaze. She would never accept the desertion of her mother. In fact, she had not ventured from this part of the wood the whole of her life. All Evangeline must do any given day was call at the border of the village and her daughter would come.

"HS," she began tentatively, "you know I cannot."

He heaved a lengthy sigh. *"This* is what you want?"

"You refer to my life? Not really, but..." An exasperated huff sent flame skittering chaotically. "You know my mother is not strong. She needs me."

"What if I need you?"

Her gaze returned to his face. "You do not need *me*. You are a god."

"The God, if you do not mind. And I do need you. More to the point, I want you. Now that those of the River's Way are all but vanished, there are few who know me upon the face of the planet Kaern, fewer still who claim my friendship. And... there is something *desperately* imperative I would like to see done." He sought her soul with his eyes. "Will you participate, Jaela?"

She blinked. "Are you sincerely claiming you want *me* for such a task—out of all the people in the world?"

With the raising of his brow, he nodded.

She returned her gaze to the tree's interior, mind racing. The proposition was unbelievably flattering, *mystifying,* but utterly impossible. "I... I could not accomplish anything for you, my friend. I am—"

"You are in no way inept, Jaela. Actually, you are chosen."

She shook her head, eyes welling with unshed tears. "After all these years, you still do not understand. I am unwanted, unaccomplished, unkempt." She pulled at a matted clump of hair. "I cannot seem to restrain these sudden urges I suffer... like that day I breathed flame into the dying babe's mouth."

"It revived him."

"But the village looks on me with even more trepidation. It is as if I am possessed."

He reflected some moments, as if perusing her spirit. "Why should you care what they think? Would they accept you any more if you had not saved the babe, if your hair was smooth, your skin cleansed, your clothes patched?"

She shook her head. "I attempted all that for years. No matter how I looked, no one but you and Mother loved me. How can people accept someone whose speech is not only muddled but makes *fire?* They find me disturbing... And I *am*."

HS sat in silence some moments before, "Have you never considered your Creator? Do you criticize my work?"

Her eyes darted back and forth between his. "I know it is you who made me this way," she answered slowly. "I... am sometimes angry with you. But..."

"But I am all you have."

"You understand my tongue," she answered with a nod. "And... you are very kind."

"I am glad you feel so. You are one of my few intimates at the moment. That is what I hope to change." He eyed her sidelong.

"Is that what you wish me to do? Find you some friends? I cannot even find one for myself."

He bobbed his head from side to side. "Something like that. Partly, anyway." He breathed a sigh. "Honestly, if I told you what I wished, you might turn me down straight out. I cannot afford that. It is judicious to allow events to unfold as time permits."

She shook her head. "I cannot—" Her tongue froze, flames cut short. Goosebumps tore down her arms. She was suffering an impulse... though it was a simple one. She must consider... *really* consider what it would mean to turn down the first request that her Creator, her best and only friend aside from her mother, had ever made of her.

Jaela stole a moment to close her eyes. She loved him.... like a father or elder brother. Certainly, he was family. More than that, he had been the best part of her life for years. She could not have born life without him. Nearly every day, she awoke, performed her household chores and spent a pleasant breakfast with her mother, all with an ache to escape to her tree and pass the time of day with this strange being. There was something uncommon about his very presence, his nearness, the way he called her friend. It did something to her soul, made her feel more than acceptable—*beautiful*, as beautiful as her lovely mother. No natural friend could make one feel thus simply by stepping into the room... or tree. HS was a *treasure*. How could she flippantly deny him when he claimed she was all he had? Quite suddenly, she felt a little sorry for him. If she was the best he could do, he must be awfully desperate.

HS chuckled at her thought. He often followed the paths of her mind, though he did not always show it. He typically worked to draw her out, to hear her speak. Considering he was the only one with whom she willingly used her voice, that meant a great deal to her.

"I admit..." he began, "you were not the first I approached. There was one other—a robust person with prowess in many areas. They would not trust that I would see them through to victory. They did not know me as you do. But please understand that they were *not* my first choice. Though you are the very best option for the journey, I knew you would be sorely tempted to turn me down."

With an almost bitter laugh, she replied, "You know me well."

"But do you not believe that I would care for you every step of the way? That no matter how things appeared, you would be in the palm of the Great One? So long as you trust him, his eyes are upon you."

Slowly, she nodded. HS always made her feel safe. He had protected her from a poisonous snake once and had hidden her from the sight of a mocking crew as they passed her tree. In countless ways, he had displayed concern and affection.

"As for falling short of ability," he resumed, "is that not for me to decide? There is nothing beyond the reach of my proficiencies. Surely, you have seen something of this. I can use anyone I please... should they be willing."

She nodded, her mind breezing through past examples of his power that were miraculous and enchanting. Was he truly so powerful? "HS?"

"Yes, love?"

"May I have some time to consider?"

His eyes burned with eagerness. "You may have all the time that passes between this moment and the opening of the path I have arranged."

"When is that?"

"You will know when the moment emerges. As for your mother, please know that, just as I shall be caring for you, so I will for her. She is not alone... She may even learn to know me again."

Her face lit up at the thought. "Mother does speak as if she dearly misses you. But she believes you cannot receive her without the cleansing of the River Lifespring."

To her surprise, his eyes bore hot flame. "I am aware of the loss she feels in making herself right before me," he answered reflectively. "That is something I am working on."

Jaela snatched at that. "What do you mean? Does it have something to do with the recompense?"

He eyed her a long while. "It does."

"Mother has never believed in it. Can you change her mind?"

"I *cannot.*"

Jaela's face dropped as her mind raced on. If she didn't know any better, she would wager he was either angry or resolute. Perhaps both, though she couldn't imagine why. After all, the forest tribes had paid the fee for the debaucheries of their peoples for as long as anyone could remember. Every annum, a young male and female from each clan, between the ages of sixteen and twenty, were selected to carry two ruby gemstones into the Nethers—the demoralizing realm where the dark one resided. These young people were what the clans called their champions.

The choice was to send their young to pay the recompense or surrender their village to be destroyed by all the powers of the Nethers. The journey was perilous—one from which the champions did not always return. The ones who did were never the same. And few were willing to describe the place to which they had ventured. Fewer still ever related any details pertaining to the quest.

"You... do not approve of the recompense?" she probed.

The flames in his eyes smoldered. "That is perhaps a tale for another time," he replied in a low rumble.

A shiver wrung through Jaela. She had never seen him so incensed. He had been angry whenever she shared tales of the village's mistreatment, but this brooding fury was utterly foreign.

"Very well," she squeaked. "I suppose I ought to return to Mother now."

He blinked and the flames dissolved. "Indeed. She is missing you."

"I will see you tomorrow then," she bid, doubtful for the first time. After all, he had asked a favor of her and she had not consented. Perhaps this was what had enraged him. "I... love you, HS." Her heart burned with the truth of it.

All at once, he was like the kindling of a fireplace on a cold evening in a bitter world. His storm gave way to tenderness as he answered, "I love you dearly, Jaela."

CHAPTER 2

ROWAN FROZE AS THE familiar voice whispered from the hollow tree, wincing as he realized where he was. He was meant to be hunting a stag for the selection ceremony to take place the following evening. He was also one of the few who was aware of where Jaela spent her afternoons. Most importantly, he was the only one who understood her tongue. This was the chief reason he avoided her, along with her hideout in the tree. It was not in his best interest that anyone should know he comprehended translations for her peculiar utterances. He was a revered citizen of the tribe, the son of one of the finest champions of the recompense. Rowan could not afford to be roped in with a supposed lunatic. Carefully, he backtracked. His expertise made certain she did not perceive his presence.

It had been due to his own blunder that he comprehended her speech. If he had not followed her into the depths of the forest those years ago, he would never have thought about her again. On that day, he had overheard a frightening commotion within her home.

"Krin," he mouthed with disgust as he recalled her father.

As a naturally inquisitive lad, he had long excelled at stealing about in order to acquire information not meant for him. He had been ten years of age when Jaela was eight. Perhaps this difference had been why his heart responded to her scream.

Racing to the window, he had peered in to discover Krin raging over his wife. She had cast her body across her daughter's. Jaela clutched her face, tears washing down her hot cheeks. When she pulled her hands away, a welt was revealed. Rowan's eyes followed the trail of bruises down her arms.

"Please, Great One," Evangeline had cried, "spare my child! Alter her course. Free her from my curse!"

Without cause, Krin fell into the chair behind him. The mother urged the girl to run to the woods, promising the father would be soothed before she returned for evening meal. The daughter did as told and Rowan could not help following. Some weakness in his young soul desired to comfort her. That had been a misstep.

Rowan now grumbled as he realized he had unconsciously traveled to the place where it had occurred. Here lay the proof of it in an arch of wild rosebushes. Jaela had fallen to her knees in a fit of tears. Rowan had crept toward her when an extraordinary light flashed from above. Its ferocity had cast him to his back and its strange weightiness held him. He'd had no choice but to watch as an extraordinary being spoke to Jaela in gentle tones that even now seemed to echo through the trees. With purpose, the entity had reached out to brush the hair from her forehead.

"Cease your weeping, dear one," it had spoken. "I am answering your mother's plea. Your course is altered. You are safe."

When the entity vanished, Rowan was free from his stranglehold on the ground. He had raced home as swiftly as his legs would carry him. It wasn't until he was safely in his cabin that he had thought to question Jaela's wellbeing. The following day, he learned her father had passed on due to a battle wound that refused to heal. Furthermore, his daughter was said to have lost her speech due to grief.

As years passed, however, not only did normal dialogue neglect to return, flames emitted from her lips. Rumors arose in consequence, but Rowan understood the truth the moment he discovered he was the only one who followed her every word. If he had been a softer person, he might have volunteered to translate for her. But he was keen enough to know better and his reputation remained as secure as his esteemed father's.

Though uncertain as to why, he now knelt down in the place he had been cast those years ago. *This* was where the peculiar personage she met each day had affected her tongue... as well as Rowan's ability to discern it. He had long known it was done of a purpose. The being entered his dreams, urging him to aid Jaela.

Problem was, she had grown into her namesake—a wild thing. It would bring dishonor upon his family to be associated with her. She possessed unpardonable quirks and rarely washed. Unlike the other girls her age, she did not groom herself to beautification—a pity since her mother was said to have been a great beauty. But unlike the graceful Evangeline, Jaela seemed scarcely human. She possessed desolate eyes shrouded in deep shadows. Her clothes were often torn and her hair was a matted, twiggy mess of what had once been willowy waves. Nay. He would not befriend her for the world.

Yet... these were not his only motivations for avoiding her. At fourteen, he had discovered his gift for stealth made it possible to get away with almost anything—especially when he was of such a family. He had taken to filching from the neighbors' larders whenever he took a fancy. Though he was not in need, he relished the sensation of taking without consequence. These behaviors had come to a screeching halt when he had spotted Jaela observing his thievery through her window. It was the first time in his life that the shame of such actions had arrested him.

Indignantly, he had abandoned his loot and hidden in the woods for the remainder of the day. It was too humiliating that the *wild thing,* of all people, had witnessed his impishness. Despite her impediment, he had been certain she would find a way to disgrace him before the whole tribe.

Days passed and nothing came of it. Either she had not been able to make her mother understand or she had opted to disregard his misdeed. Even so, the sight of her always brought his guilt to mind. He loathed that someone knew he was not what everyone believed, that he was not a man of honor like his father, that he was easily tempted into evils. He had since run from that side of his nature as best he could in order to become worthy of his reputation.

"What are you doing sitting about, you lazy oaf?" his younger sister abruptly chided with bow in hand as she entered the clearing in which he reminisced. "Here is our best tracker sitting on his *behind* while we have been honored with the task of hunting the ceremonial stag."

Rowan leaped to his feet, shaking the memories back into the past. "I was listening," he answered. It was his highly perceptive ears that made him the best of the trackers. He had learned to sit in silence.

"I would like to see you try that one on Father. Your lady-friend has made bets on you winning our prey, so you had best get moving."

"My *what?*"

"Oh, do not tell me you are unaware that the beautiful Caspa has laid claim to you. Give it an annum or two and you shall be living happily ever after."

He snorted. "You have no idea how many have tried it, Briar. I will not be tied down until I am good and ready." He was a man of twenty years who appreciated the possibilities before him. He was not going to settle for anything short of the worthiest path... once he discovered what that was.

"I forgot what a lady's man you are," Briar answered. "I thank you for reminding me. Now, may we return to our venture?"

With the rolling of his eyes, Rowan took up his longbow and retreated into the trees. He must cease all remembrances concerning Jaela the Wild Thing.

CHAPTER 3

JAELA ENTERED THE SINGLE-ROOM log dwelling to find Evangeline sitting cross-legged before the fireplace, gazing into its flames. At the creak of the door's closing, her mother peered up with a welcoming smile.

"I thought I would have to excuse myself for evening meal," she commented. "Cannot bear to go without you."

Taking a seat beside her mother, Jaela cast a thoughtful glance about the room. The notion of leaving even for a short time made her stomach turn. This was their serenity, where none dared tread. The scent of dried flowers blended with that of fresh herbs and plants was home. Since Evangeline prized privacy, theirs was the only dwelling to possess window coverings, which contributed to the coziness of the place. The large fur cushion upon which they sat was their place of comfort, accentuated by her mother's handwoven blanket.

Evangeline was an expert of woven wares. It was one of the rare skills of the river people. None else was knowledgeable of her craft, making it notable to possess a piece of her work. This put the Tribe of Deerskin on the map for exports, which furthered the tribe's forbearance concerning her presence among them.

It was forgotten by all but herself that she had only been spared death to be wedded to Warrior Krin. Against her will, she had been united with the very tribe who had destroyed her whole way of life. She had been torn from a culture of tranquility and purity for that of coarseness and bloodshed. And when her husband had found her affection impossible to win, he reviled her. It wasn't long before years of cruelty commenced. Jaela was four years of age when she witnessed the first occurrence. She had attempted to stop him, but he'd cast her aside as if she were a feather.

Jaela had often wondered why the Great One allowed one of his own to enter into such a state of affairs. One day, Evangeline had read the question in her eyes and taken the blame upon herself. "We all possess free will, Jaela. I had opportunity to run before the ceremony. Fear pinned me."

Jaela had searched her mother with astonishment.

"If I had trusted upon the Great One, upon the teachings of my upbringing, I would have fled and he would have cared for me. But... after everything that happened to my people, trepidation gripped my soul." She turned to her daughter with remorseful eyes. "I chose to go through with the ceremony. All I wanted at the time was to see my needs met... even if it was by the very people who had slain my own..." She swallowed. "I was the cause of my curse."

This had sent Jaela reeling. To think her mother felt she could have lived a whole other life if only she had not been so afraid. Yet, she could in no way blame her. She could not imagine enduring what Evangeline had.

"But... in his immense mercy," Evangeline continued, "the Great One sent me a consolation prize. Though I went years without conceiving, he eventually sent me you, my own little angel. I do not know where I would be without you."

It wasn't until Jaela had reached eight years of age that Krin had harmed her mother's beloved daughter—the very child he had broodingly loathed because she was part river people. The occurrence that day had led to the birth of Jaela's disorder. Krin had not lived another full day. And in acquiring the friendship of the Great One, she had lost that of all else. She told herself it was worth it, but her scorned existence was difficult to cope with for someone of her sensitive nature.

Her mother bore the unspoken alienation between them and the clan with grace—a true follower of the River's Way. Jaela wished she had been raised in such an environment. Evangeline insisted Jaela's language was much like that of the angelic species who used to visit her people from time to time, though few had possessed the eye to see them. If this was so, the river people might have accepted her tongues.

Now, as Evangeline sipped her steaming kempur while gazing into the hearth, she spoke wistfully, "He is very good about sending you back to me, is he not?" It was as if she spoke of an estranged father.

Jaela studied her mother, whose appearance was striking, even without the River Lifespring's power. The daughter had long wished she had inherited Evangeline's features instead of her father's, as many had voiced over the years. It was difficult not to feel reduced in the presence of one so lovely, especially when the woman claimed she was centuries older than her appearance indicated.

Jaela had forsaken her own appearance for many years. It mattered little how she looked. Her people could not accept her. Therefore, her hair was matted, her face often smudged and her clothes ill-kept. Evangeline seemed to understand. And despite her beauty, she was not one to concern herself with appearances. Her people had maintained that the real beauty of a person lay in their heart.

It made Jaela ache that Evangeline believed HS could not receive her as a friend. It was illogical when Jaela had never touched the River Lifespring and she met with him every day. But her mother insisted Jaela's case was special. She believed her daughter's miraculous touch from the Great One made her practically immortal. But Jaela knew better. She was well acquainted with her inner turmoil, that she often hated her people, despite the fact her mother deemed such sentiment iniquitous. Jaela was soulish enough for any human, even under her virtuous mother's instruction.

Evangeline was something of a saint herself. She could not simply receive the allotted bounty due her place as the widow of an honored one. Living by a code all her own, she covertly shared her portion with those in need and fabricated clothes for those who had little.

Once, she had overheard the comely Caspa—Jaela's greatest tormentor—insist upon mortification if she could not get something new for that year's Selection Ceremony. Evangeline spent that evening developing a fresh garment, leaving it on the girl's doorstep before sunrise. This had angered Jaela more than she could have spoken if she were capable. She stomped about for days until her mother sat her down in order to clarify her actions.

"Though I am no longer worthy of it," she explained, "I serve a special kingdom, not of this world. The ways of my people were different from all else. We received a singular mandate from the Great One. Though I am separated from him and my people are quite gone, I cannot bring myself to forsake our ways."

She had proceeded to take a package from behind her back and lay it in Jaela's hands. With irritation, Jaela had untied the strings and pulled back the covering to discover a dress even lovelier than the one that had been made for her enemy. The ice in her heart melted as she sprang into her mother's arms. Though she could not fathom Evangeline's heart, she treasured it.

Evangeline broke into Jaela's revelry by standing from her place before the hearth. "Shall we be going? You know how they stare when we are late." With a gleam, she added, "Poor dears have not any better interest than to be bemused by us meager souls."

Jaela forced a smile. She loathed the evening meals. The entire village gathered around bonfires with all the comradery of family. For so long, she had ached to feel part of it. They would not share a fire with the wild thing. Yet, it was nearly prohibited to miss. Evangeline felt it was a small price to pay in order to avoid drumming up further discord.

The drums met Jaela with rare pleasure as they neared the dining region. She determined it must be young Alfri performing. Though he was the newest drummer, his rhythms charmed her more than the others. At a mere twelve years, he was the youngest ever to be bestowed the responsibility. The lad caught the half-smile on her face, casting her one of his knowing nods. Though it was no secret how people responded to his music, he seemed especially gratified to have moved the speechless girl. It was a small prize to her, for most did not care for her good opinion.

There were numerous galmoira present this night. The small, winged creatures served as lanterns for evening festivities. The night provoked their glow as they hung from the yellow moss of the trees. Jaela had always been fond of the animal, regarding them as stars from the heavens come to visit upon their humble village.

She and Evangeline took their seats beside Elder Si. Tales of him went so far back that Jaela surmised he must be nearing a hundred years of age. He had been tribe leader of Deerskin at one time, as well as a great warrior who had possessed unique wisdom and a keen sense of justice. There had even been peace between Deerskin and the river people in his time. Those days were long behind them and he had grown into something of a village recluse, who remained nearly as silent as Jaela. Yet, he always spared a few words for Evangeline. So, they sat with him in their silent corner on the edge of the bonfires, where few ventured.

"Celestial twilight, Si," Evangeline greeted as they sat upon the tree stumps that encircled his fire.

Si nodded. He did not typically waste words on mere pleasantries. If he spoke, it was for a purpose, even if one could not always perceive it. Whether or not Jaela could, her mother always did. This was likely the reason she was a favorite with him. Moreover, she wove him a fresh garment every annum at the time of the Celestial Festivities. That was the only instance that Jaela ever saw him smile.

The Celestial Festivities occurred once an annum, always overlapping with the Time of Recompense. Glorious, rainbow-like phenomenon glowed in the evening sky in ethereal hues over the course of three evenings. Accompanying the event were ancient prophecies pertaining to a hero who would one day emerge to eradicate the requirements of the recompense. This liberator was due to appear during a Celestial Spectacle. Ergo, the clans traditionally celebrated his forthcoming arrival with extravagant dance recitals, choral performances, the playing of traditional games and the giving and receiving of gifts.

Upon the final evening, a grand feast of birds and swine were spiced with piquant seasonings and slow-roasted to perfection.

Every fruit and vegetable available at the time played attendance. Certainly not least of the food prepared was a dessert made from ground chiro fruit expertly combined with goat's milk. The dish was brown as soil but rich as a king's bounty. Jaela could not help relishing this time of year for the satisfaction of the delicacy.

After a satisfying supper of fresh fish roasted from a skewer, Jaela nibbled the remainder as the evening recital commenced. This typically began with the young ribbon dancers. The elder dancers were reserved for special occasions. The dancing was often followed by a musical performance, preferably vocal.

There were a rare few among the tribes who possessed the ancient gift of voice. Their song sent objects to flight, increased the growth of crops, affected the weather and so on. Jaela wished her speech possessed such effect. She would be valued rather than despised. Although she liked to sing on occasion, it always emerged in her strange language and with no result but the fearful flame.

After a pleasant vocal arrangement, they reached the duels. These took place between warriors young and old as they tested and ranked themselves before the entire tribe. Jaela did not typically pay much heed to this, instead sneaking home for an early sleep.

With a nod to her mother, she prepared to do so when Rowan took to the center of the arena. For as long as she could recall, he had excelled in combat of every kind. His talent was less gruesome and more like a dance as he bequeathed little harm to his adversaries. This was in no way traditional to the tribes.

Jaela had long questioned if this was because he possessed a more sympathetic nature than he would have others believe.

This evening was no different. No one proved a match for him except his own sister. When they competed with their bows, it was impossible to tell which was the better marksman. The two, along with their father, made the family famous for their prowess.

Jaela had long admired the sister. She was brave, outspoken and quick as a whip. Of all the girls she might wish for a friend, it was her. But even if Jaela weren't an enigma, she was no kind of companion for such a girl. If Jaela was meek as a mouse, Briar was formidable as a bear.

As the contests concluded, the tribespeople prepared to return to the warmth of their homes when Tribe Leader Baron's voice sounded over the crowd. "A moment, please," he appealed, "I have a final pronouncement." He waited some moments while the villagers returned to their seats. "As you are aware, we draw near the Celestial Festivities."

Applause and cheering resounded. After a moment, he threw out his hands for silence, which swiftly followed. No one dared dishonor the clan leader.

"We anticipate this time of year," Baron continued with a nod, "but we cannot neglect the traditional recompense that arrives hand in hand."

As if any could forget the significant occasion. No one wished to be reminded, especially those within the age range. Not only was it torturous to envision being selected as champion, it was never pleasant to recall the obligation that derived from their debaucheries. It was because they were an impure and deficient people that two of their children must be sent into the Nethers once an annum.

"Tomorrow evening," Baron continued somberly, "a pair of champions, between the ages of sixteen and twenty, will be supernaturally selected to carry the recompense into the very core of the Nethers. We now request that every young person within the range line up to lay their lips upon the time-honored ruby in order to relay their willingness to complete the commission... though it may cost so much as their very lives." He swallowed before raising his chin to assert, "Any unwilling to perform this ceremony will be cast from the tribes forevermore."

Jaela swallowed as she watched the others take their place in line. It was a large responsibility for the young. Some actually appeared eager for the chance to prove themselves, to become one of those to return with legendary tales of prowess. Most were mournful or terrified. The rest were merely surrendered to the possibility of selection.

Jaela's mother eyed her sidelong. She did not nudge her on. Though her daughter may live in disgrace, she would not shrink from her duty. With a sigh, Jaela stood to take her place at the end of the line.

Briar, Rowan's sister, drew up behind her. She was laughing with her father over some confidential jest before he moved on to speak with others. Jaela had not realized she was staring until the girl met her eyes.

"I am not late due to fear," Briar asserted bluntly. "I was just closing a conversation with my father."

Jaela nodded her understanding. Truth be told, she had not doubted the girl a moment. She was simply accustomed to considering people without their ever noticing.

Briar relaxed into a casual, wide-legged stance. To Jaela's surprise, she continued quietly, "Are you worried?"

Jaela eyed her. Yes, she was. But dared she admit it with even so much as a nod?

Briar nodded herself, seeming to have read Jaela's thoughts. "Everyone is. Me? I have been praying to the celestial *wonders* for this chance every annum since my maturity."

Jaela nodded again. She had no doubt. Briar would make the perfect heroine of legend.

When they had nearly reached the moment of concession, Briar leaned in to whisper, "I hear if you scarcely graze the gem, it neglects to register you. Almost everyone does it."

Jaela stole a step back. She understood that Briar meant it good-naturedly. But Jaela could not help being affronted by the assumption that she possessed so little honor. Certainly, she was meek as a mouse, but she had integrity.

With a slow-burning fire in her eyes, Jaela stepped up to the emerald green cushion upon which the large ruby lay. She had been here before. She'd survived it. The likelihood of her selection was minute. Even so, she acknowledged the chance she would be chosen. And she must show this girl she was no coward.

Taking the ruby into her hands, she turned to the side to reveal her profile to the formidable Briar. Without hesitation, she put her lips to it, utterly yielding herself to its prospects. Briar responded with a mollified smile. Though bestowed but momentarily, Jaela left with the hope that perhaps she had gained some measure of respect from one member of her tribe. For once, she met her mother with head held high.

CHAPTER 4

"HS," Jaela's heart called, though what emerged from her lips might have been anything.

The hollow tree remained in darkness, silence. This was the first time in years that he neglected to appear. She knew why. He had made a request and she had yet to make up her mind. He offered her room do so.

Her thoughts toiled. She *could not* leave her mother. Everything in her raged against it. But what would he do or say if she refused? Would she spend the remainder of her life wondering what she had missed? Intimate friend or not, this was the essence of the Creator of all things entreating her. What happened when one turned down such a personage? And would it break her heart to do so?

Yes.

Tears of frustration streamed down her cheeks. *What can I do?* she mused. *I cannot go! Why would he ask it of me?*

He knew her through in through. He was her ultimate—nay, her *only*—confidante. He understood her fears, shortcomings, relationship with her mother and that Evangeline would be utterly alone without her. The woman could not boast the friendship of the Creator for comfort.

The concept of venturing into unknown places terrified the living starlight out of her. Yet... she *was* intrigued, even drawn, to the opportunity. She had never known the world outside her wood. She had not even visited other clans, for who would want her? But in her mother's youth, she had traveled far and wide. And Jaela had overheard tales from the village elders. Sometimes their accounts boded great peril, while others astonishing wonder.

Such recollections raced through her mind as she exited the hollow tree. Quiet as a deer, she strolled the forest. She was always careful to avoid her people. So, it was with astonishment that she suddenly faced Rowan.

They froze in the small clearing, silently facing one another. It seemed ages passed before his mouth opened as if he would speak. Finally, he closed it and passed on with a nod.

Jaela was left in confusion. Now and then, she encountered others like this. But few considered speaking to her. Only the evening before, Briar had done just that. Now, her brother had nearly greeted Jaela before his better judgement sent him on.

The snapping of a twig made her spin about. Rowan stood with a hand to his neck.

"Look..." he began before faltering. The next moment, he ended, "Er, celestial fortune this evening."

Before she could think of a way to respond, he turned and marched on.

A corner of her lips curled up as she watched him disappear. She could not fathom the cause of his friendliness. He had avidly avoided her since she had witnessed his thievery some years back. She had certainly not held it against him, nor had she ever snitched. But she perceived it made him uncomfortable to have her know. So, what had caused this breech today? Had Briar mentioned Jaela's courage?

Her stomach dropped. What courage did she possess? She had faced the kissing of a stone, but how did she respond when her best friend in all the universe summoned her to a journey? It was true that by embracing the gem, she had surrendered herself to just such a possibility—a treacherous expedition into the very realm of The Nethers, from which some never returned. But she had not *really* believed she would be selected. HS *had* selected her, from all the people in all the world. It was an unsurpassable distinction. Only a coward would turn it down.

Evangeline smiled as Jaela entered their dwelling. "Did you enjoy your time?"

Jaela tried to smile back but gave way to the shaking of her head.

Her mother appeared shocked. "Why ever not, dear heart?"

Jaela shrugged, holding up a hand to insinuate she was unwilling to attempt conveying her troubles.

"Are you... anxious about this evening?"

Jaela rolled her eyes. What did she care of the selection ceremony when she had discovered just how small she was? She could not even venture to travel with HS, let alone into the Nethers. The ruby had seen her through and through. It knew better than to look to her for the tribe's salvation.

Evangeline seated herself beside her daughter as the fire labored under their gazes. Jaela absently stoked it with a poker.

"Did he not come?" Evangeline asked softly.

Jaela shook her head.

"I see... But this has happened before. He turned up again."

Jaela shrugged.

"You have no idea how very favored you are, my daughter. You are the most fortunate girl in all the world to share such companionship with the spirit of the Great One. You must not take that for granted. You are chosen, Jaela."

Jaela leaped to her feet. She did not need to be reminded of how special her encounters with HS were. She needed her mother to tell her he would understand when she told him no. That could be her only answer. She had faced herself. She was yellow.

She felt the warmth of her mother's hand on her back. The softness of it brought tears to her eyes. *This.* This was worth staying for.

Evangeline turned Jaela's chin to face her gaze. "What is it?"

Jaela did not possess the words to respond. Not that she could if she wished. Instead, she threw her arms around Evangeline and held her tight. She was *glad* to be staying right here with the only human who loved her. They were all each other had.

"Very well," Evangeline answered with a sigh. "It will keep. Just know how much I love my sweet angel. You are... so *precious*, Jaela."

Jaela squeezed tighter, basking in the security of such love. If HS withdrew from her, this was all she had in the world. But it was *warm* and safe.

⟶⟩⟩⟩ ⟨⟨⟨⟵

Jaela went through the motions of the evening banquet without tasting anything. She felt no satisfaction, too numb from her self-realizations as well as fear she would lose HS. Though it hardly concerned her, she dreaded the Selection Ceremony as well. It was just another reminder of her newly discovered shortcoming.

The usual entertainment was exchanged for official proceedings. The tension was palpable. This was the only ritual that did not transpire for pleasure's sake. It was an obligation that had been endured for generations.

At the center of the bonfires was a larger configuration of logs prepared only from trees that grew along the River Lifespring. Though they had lost their supernatural effect, the wood still lit with eagerness that proved they had once possessed miraculous substance. Tribe Leader Baron ignited it from the tip of a long baton. Instantly, it was pure white blaze. Gasps and sighs sounded over the spectacle.

The cushion containing the ruby gemstone was delivered by another of the tribe leaders. Tribe Leader Baron carefully seized the gem with a set of tongs. Lifting it above the flames, he stole a moment to regard his audience. With a brow raised, he seemed to ask, *"Are we ready?"*

The ruby was released. In a flash of light, the flames transformed—jade at the base, followed by cerulean with covert wisps of violet and rose. Gasps followed, along with an appreciative stomping of feet. Though all dreaded the ceremony that would commence, no one could help admiring this phenomenon.

Jaela was always struck by its hues so incongruent to that of a typical flame. The fire that emerged from her mouth did so in similar variance. Her mother had often compared it with the hues of the Celestial Spectacle. Jaela couldn't help wondering what made both her fire and this one so unusual.

"Creator of the flame," the tribe leader began in his reverberating voice, "who do you elect to carry the rightful recompense on behalf of the Tribe of Deerskin?"

For some moments, nothing occurred. It was as if the Creator had yet to make up his mind. Meanwhile, the stomachs of children, parents and grandparents toiled.

"Jaela."

She leaped and searched wildly for her friend, wondering if others had heard. She neither discovered him nor that anyone else had perceived his voice.

HS? she answered in her mind, heart pounding. He had never spoken to her apart from their communion in the forest.

"Have you formed your determination?" he asked. "Will you go for me?"

The pounding of her heart filled her ears. She had led a simple life. She knew her tribe and her village. Not much frightened her in her small world. This question did.

Oh, HS, she whimpered inwardly. She wished he would not ask her, especially at a time like this. With abruptness, the impossible occurred to her.

Are you... asking if I am willing to be chosen to deliver the recompense?

"Aye."

Her body felt faint. To go out into the world for him was asking enough... but to face *the Nethers?*

I... she began. The tongue of her heart would not move. She tried and tried again, but something stopped her. What was it?

Tribe Leader Baron cleared his throat. The process was taking longer than usual. It was plain that he was uncomfortable. "Creator of flame, who will you send?" he shouted.

Love, Jaela realized. It was love that stopped her. She worshipped this friend so sincerely that she did not possess the ability to turn him down. Pressing her eyelids shut, she clenched her fists to her heart.

I am willing, she told him.

A white burst of flame escaped the ceremonial fire. The flickering tongue drifted over the crowd. Many ducked in trepidation. To Jaela's astonishment, it started toward her but moved on. It hesitated over Rowan and Briar before disappearing into the crown of Rowan's head. The process did not appear painful, though the widening of his eyes revealed he felt something. Without hesitation, he stood to his feet to indicate he accepted the choosing. He would represent his tribe for the rightful recompense.

Jaela released a sigh of relief. Perhaps HS had only been testing her. After all, the flame had almost seemed to want Briar. The brother and sister would make a fearsome team. The likelihood of legendary status was high.

She swallowed a cry as the second flame blasted toward her without reservation. The absorption made her go warm all over. With the eyes of the entire village upon her, she forced herself upon trembling legs. In the next moment, they buckled and her vision was engulfed by darkness.

CHAPTER 5

"I CANNOT *BELIEVE* THE pathetic little creature *fainted!*" Briar growled.

Rowan offered a half-smile as he packed his belongings. It was customary to begin the journey upon the day that followed the choosing. But it was difficult to get anything accomplished this night alongside his sister's outcries.

"Do not smirk at me like that, Rowan!" she reprimanded. "You *know* something went wrong. How could a girl like that ever help you... *or* protect you?!"

Rowan placed burly fists on his hips. "I do not require protecting, baby sister."

She crossed her arms disbelievingly. "Even if that were so, you are expected to protect *her*. She will hold you back if you can even get her there and back again in one piece. A quest with the wild thing certainly will not make a hero of you."

"I beg to differ," he answered. "I will return all the more valiant with a defenseless damsel in tow."

He knew he had won the point when Briar cracked a smile.

"I do not like it, Rowan," she persisted. "I should be at your side. I wanted this. She, *clearly*, did not."

"That will be enough, Briar," their father interrupted as he stepped into the room. "We must trust the choosing. It is a disgrace to speak otherwise."

"Even if we *do* harbor doubts," added their mother as she stood beside her husband.

The husband turned to her for a moment, questioning her admission, then returned his gaze to Rowan. Striding across the floor, he placed hands on the shoulders of his son. "There was none more worthy than you to be chosen, my son. You will easily follow in my footsteps."

Rowan twitched, though none took notice. It was true that, physically, he was the tribe's best bet. But to be worthy was another matter. *Was* he worthy? He knew his shortcomings, his history. He had tried to live as honorably as his revered parents but possessed a strain of roguishness that had been difficult to eliminate. Yet, what did worthiness have to do with it? There was none so gifted in warfare as he among all of Deerskin.

"I thank you, Father," he answered. "I will work hard to make you and Mother—*even Briar*—proud."

"I reserve no doubts on that score," the father replied, removing his hands to follow his wife from the room.

Rowan's gaze shot to his sister. As he had feared, she appeared wounded.

"You know he would have said the same about you," he tried.

"Would not," she spat. "I am no son."

"They are proud of you nonetheless."

She shook her head. "Maybe. But nothing I do will ever be enough to make me equal to you in their eyes."

Rowan blinked. "Is that... why you wanted to go? To prove your merit?"

The reddening of her face revealed he had hit his mark. "No one could belittle me after returning from the recompense unscathed," she admitted.

Rowan ran a hand through his hair, sympathizing for his closest comrade. "I almost wish you could go in my place—"

"You do not."

"—because I *know* you would prove to everyone what you are made of."

Her eyes flicked to his. "You do not mean that, Ro."

"I do," he replied with conviction. "Why do you think I let you hang around with me all these years? No one else could keep up. And you are two years my junior. Imagine if we were of the same age. You are a force to be reckoned with, Briar of Deerskin."

He was astonished to witness the watering of her eyes. This selection had meant more to her than he had realized. The esteem of their parents was a deep desire and was no simple feature to garner. Though they publicly embraced Briar's typically-boyish ways, they privately preferred she would follow after someone like Caspa's example. Strong women were admired within the clans, but a girl who could best the boys was an anomaly they scarcely knew what to do with. Problem was, Rowan had long been her idol. He had liked having her around. Therefore, he taught her his ways and she had excelled.

"Perhaps..." she began with trembling voice. Clearing her throat, she continued, "Perhaps I will get my chance one day."

Rowan shut his mouth as he returned to his packing. Though it was true he was more than happy to be chosen himself, he did not truly relish the notion of one day sending Briar. He had heard things about this journey that she had not. Like their father, their great-grandfather had been selected and lived to tell about it. From what Rowan had learned, the Nethers was the last place he would send anyone he loved.

It was why having Jaela along made things complicated. He did not love her as he did Briar of course—far from it. But she was in no way prepared for what lay ahead. It was sure to require all his prowess to keep them both safe. It would be a true test of his abilities. If the girl in question were not so thin-skinned and petite, he wouldn't bat an eye. But he was certain she would make a true damsel in distress.

The fact he was the only person who could comprehend her strange speech did not escape his concern. It was a little too ideal that a peculiarly-tongued girl and the only one who could translate had been selected together. There was a good chance that the Creator of flame had done it for a purpose. This was why he would not outwardly complain about his traveling companion. He was the only one who understood there was more at play than readily met the eye, but only time would tell.

The following morning, Jaela sat in customary silence while Evangeline brushed her dark hair into glistening waves. The mother had insisted Jaela be thoroughly scrubbed the evening before and now spent eons working her hair into order. Jaela cared very little for the task aside from her mother's care. This made her treasure the process. Though Evangeline did not value the outward appearance, this ordeal was another matter. As she had explained, she saw the merit of sending her daughter into the world adorned in her best armor. Jaela would meet those who did not know her as their village did. First impressions were everything now. Therefore, she presented her daughter with the finest garments in her arsenal, packing the comb into her pack with the instruction to keep tidy for her mother's sake.

Side by side, they traversed the village paths. It had been agreed between Evangeline and Rowan's parents that Jaela meet Rowan at his esteemed home after morning meal. What Jaela had not expected were the throngs that surveyed them. Was this done every annum? Perhaps so, but she doubted they typically looked upon the champions with such skepticism. She was the village freak, after all. She could not blame them.

Little did they know, she had chosen this course. They might have had better representation, but she had declined to deny her friend. She could not help wondering if it had been the same for Rowan and wished she could inquire. But there lay her complicated tongue in the way.

"It matters not what they think," Evangeline murmured. "Never has. They do not possess discernment."

Jaela had heard this from her mother for so long that it ceased to possess meaning. Especially when all she was surrounded with every day of her life was the picture others had painted for her. The village denied their approval. She had endured under it for a decade.

What she really wished to know was what HS had been thinking. Why had he chosen *her* for this unpleasant task? It seemed to her that anyone else would have been worthier of the place beside Rowan.

And what of her daily rendezvous with HS? Would she be denied them on this expedition? She wasn't certain she could do without. They were life's blood. Perhaps he would continue to speak to her as he had at the ceremony, breathing words into her mind that none else could hear.

At long last, they drew near Rowan's home. The structure was of considerable size for that of Deerskin. It signified his father's prosperous life. The man was so accomplished that many jested he could walk on water. Surrounding the front stoop was a prestigious company. Jaela ascertained they were present to see their champions off. Her stomach toiled as she neared.

Rowan's parents emerged from the dwelling to greet those assembled. Rowan soon followed with what appeared to be a whole armistice strapped upon his person. The lad certainly looked formidable. This comforted Jaela. If she must go, at least it was with the very best of the clan's warriors.

To her surprise, Rowan's eye met none but hers. She searched for the misgivings she had noted in others. He merely nodded a greeting. Either he was a fair actor or he might actually believe she would make a capable companion. Confidence flowed into her bones until she recalled he really did not need her. He was *Rowan*, son of the dauntless Bowan. She was merely his companionable dog.

As Jaela and Evangeline entered the crowd, Rowan's mother graciously stepped forward.

"Jaela, daughter of the honorable Krin," she greeted, placing an arm about her.

Jaela wondered if her eyes bulged as wide as they felt. This was nothing like the greetings she typically received. She lifted the corner of her mouth in a side-smile as the mothers exchanged acknowledgments.

Unexpectedly, the woman escorted her to the stoop where Rowan stood. Together, the champions faced the company. A kind of ceremony commenced. Blessings and words of counsel were pronounced. The recompense was served in the form of a pair of rubies to be presented by each of them. But both were passed to Rowan in a secure satchel.

Jaela found it difficult to focus on what was said. She was too distracted by the realization that Rowan was almost a foot taller than her. She must look a child beside him, though he was but two years older. This presentation served only to mortify her. It was not in her they placed their hopes but the strapping warrior beside her. She was not so much his dog as a sore thumb.

Finally, they stepped from the stoop to shake hands with the company and pay final farewells. Most of these were exchanged with Rowan while Jaela watched on. But as sudden as a bolt of lightning, Elder Si was beside her.

"Beware the malicious sprites what inhabits the open forestry," he spoke soberly, piercing her eyes with his own. "Take heed of them what lurks in shadows, prowling like ravenous beasts in search of them what may be devoured. They..." He swallowed, eyes shooting back and forth between hers with restrained emotion. "They *revile* our peoples and do not truly desire the recompense, child, but our destruction. Should you succeed in payin' it... it is accomplished at too great a price." He grasped her hand, even going so far as to stroke it with his thumb as if she were his own kin. "It is *too high,* wee Jaela. And it is too late for me... Tiz a curse what darkens the remainder of a life no matter how swift one runs."

Chills swept through Jaela as she stared back at him. Uncertain of how to respond to such dire cautions, she merely nodded. She wished she could inquire further. Malicious sprites? Could he mean the daemons that dwelled in the Nethers, to which they must now journey? It was difficult enough to imagine entering their region. Must she fear them every step of the way? How would she ever make it? Especially when they apparently did not even wish her to accomplish the mission. But the recompense was an arrangement made between the ancient clans and the dark one centuries prior. Surely, it must be honored by both contingents?

With a somberness deeper still, Elder Si caught Rowan in his gaze. "Watch out for our firetongue, lad. She is worth far more than rubies... Our people *do not know.*"

Rowan's brows rose as he cast a swift glance to Jaela. She had not realized *she* was the "firetongue" until then, nor had she ever imagined the reserved elder retained a special term for her. Was it of his own devising? Or, by some fabulous chance, had he heard of people like her before? If only.

With a final squeeze to her hand, Elder Si abandoned the gathering. Jaela's eyes searched his back. The man of few words had come only to present these warnings. It sent a shiver through her. Ultimately, the question that played through her mind was how her worth could possibly be more than rubies, a girl who could not even speak rightly.

These questions were forsaken as she observed Rowan's irregular behavior. They had neared the end of the crowd when she realized he was in search of someone. It was clear he could not locate them and was torn between apprehension and pain. Before she realized it, he had observed her inquisitive glance.

"Er..." he hesitated. "I am wondering what is keeping Briar. We... have not made our farewells."

"What is it, Rowan?" his father questioned upon overhearing the quiet panic in his voice.

"Where is Briar?"

Bowan's face clouded as he scanned the crowd. "You have not seen her this morning?"

Rowan shook his head.

The father exchanged words with his wife. When he returned his attention to Rowan, it was to explain with irritation, "I am afraid you must go forth, my son. It will appear cowardly to stall. I will relay your farewell to your sister."

Jaela's stomach dropped for Rowan. She knew why Briar was missing. His sister was angry that she had not been chosen in Jaela's place. She had been so eager, even willing to speak with the wild thing about it. Jaela had stolen her place.

She felt her world would cave in with shame before a warm hand pressed upon her back. She turned to find her mother beside her. She knew both their hearts were breaking with this first separation, especially under the circumstances. Despite the surveying crowd, Jaela flew into Evangeline's arms. It looked childish, she knew, but she could not help it. She told herself that every moment stolen with her mother bought Rowan time to watch for Briar. Surely, his sister would not truly abandon him at such an hour.

"The Great One will watch over you, Jaela," Evangeline whispered into her ear. "He always has."

Jaela pulled away. Perhaps he would, but he was also the one calling her to leave. Yet, he was her only comfort. He would not draw her onto such a path only to abandon her... would he?

It nearly stole the breath from her when Rowan started resolutely down the path that led out of the village. They were really doing this, *leaving*, traveling to the Nethers—the den of death itself. It was the very place where the souls of the dead were supposed to reside for eternity, where daemonkind ruled and the lover of darkness himself plotted wicked devices. This... was their destination.

Traipsing after Rowan, Jaela shook such thoughts from her mind. It was too much. She must take one step at a time, such as focusing on her reluctant departure.

It wasn't until they entered the glowing quiet of the forest that Jaela recalled the champion beside her. His jaw was tightly clenched. Could it be he was unhappy to go as well? To go with *her?* Perhaps. But she knew better. He mourned Briar's absence at the ceremony. She was the one with whom he had been thick as thieves all their lives. How Jaela wished she could offer some comfort.

In the next moment, he was glancing down at her. As if reading her mind, he seemed to force his face to relax. "She will get over it," he said with a sigh. "And I will see her again upon our return."

Though his tone was light, she surmised he felt no better. It was said for her benefit, though why he cared that she was burdened was beyond her. For that matter, why *was* she? She supposed she had always been that way. She was a sympathetic girl from whom none desired sympathy.

"That elder," he began suddenly, "the one who sits with you and your mother at evening meals..."

Her eyes flew to his face. He knew where she sat? Of course, he did. She was the freak of the village. She nodded.

"He is Si, a former tribe leader of Deerskin, is he not?"

She nodded again, wondering what he was getting at.

"He is a past champion as well, if I remember correctly."

She cast her gaze to the path, wishing he would drop the subject. She wanted to believe that the sage elder had merely been prattling folklore.

"Do you... do you believe he spoke true?" he questioned. "I mean, about the malevolent sprites?"

Her mind raced. She had spent time in the forestry near their village. Rowan had, as well. Clearly, neither of them was acquainted with what Elder Si had spoken of. In conclusion, she shrugged.

CHAPTER 6

As THE SUN ROSE higher in the sky, Rowan concluded they must soon take time to eat and rest. This would give him time to determine their course. They had been afforded a map that marked the recommended route, along with instructions as to which clans were and were not prudent to visit. It would be wise to acquaint himself with the entirety. More importantly, he desired to get his mind off Briar. She had understood how significant the occasion was. She had desired the opportunity as much as he. This disloyalty seemed to suck all the glory out of it.

And what if, heaven forbid, he shouldn't return? She would certainly mourn her choice, for he knew she loved him at least half as much as he did her. They had often considered the possibility that they cared more for one another than even their own parents did. For reasons beyond the siblings, their mother and father were not altogether warm people. Appearances were the crux of their lives and their aspirations reached even beyond their current prestige. Yet, the two agreed they had been fortunate in their parentage. They had been well cared for all their lives and appreciated everything afforded them.

"Seems like we should stop to eat... you agree?" he asked distractedly, scanning for a good stopping place.

Jaela nodded, though it seemed to him she would rather continue. He gathered she wanted to complete this mission with haste in order to return to her mother. He could not blame her. At the moment, he felt similarly, which was unsatisfactory. This was the opportunity he had been waiting for—a chance to prove himself a champion of the clans, like his father and great-grandfather before him.

He soon seated them beside a dawdling brook within the shade of a resplendent weeping willow. They had each been provided a pack of supplies at the farewell ceremony. How long they would last was yet to be determined. The pair may need to consider careful rationing. But for now, his companion appeared too weary to be faced with such a suggestion. Would she ever not be?

After breaking into his supply of smoked venison, he surveyed her warily. She was even paler than usual, so short and reedy. He considered the fact that she had never been trained in warfare. Could she survive the quest beside him?

When her eyes timidly lifted, he averted his gaze. To cover his embarrassment, he said, "Mother packed a bundle of seedcakes for me. Care for one?"

She shook her head. It was then he realized she was making a mere show of eating. The poor girl was either too fatigued or too frightened to entertain an appetite.

He passed her a cake. "This is a lengthy journey. It may be several days before we reach the Nethers. You will need all the strength you can muster."

With a nod, she accepted it. Her eyes shone with thankfulness upon her first bite. There was nothing like Mother's practiced cooking to ease a troubled spirit. But what was he to do with such a vulnerable girl? He must be on constant guard for their safety, plotting several steps ahead.

In reality, he was on his own here, save what company this mute afforded. Of course... they could speak back and forth if he were willing to divulge his secret. That was not an option. What would be the use of returning a hero when everyone discovered him in converse with—what had Elder Si called her—a *firetongue?*

Rowan was refilling their waterskins when something snapped in the forest behind them. It was clear Jaela had not caught it. Moving unconcernedly so as not to worry her, he examined their surroundings. In the end, he deduced it had been a rabbit or fox. Perhaps even a deer. He was more easily spooked due to that elder's yarns. Yet, the hairs on the back of his neck stood on end and he made certain his longbow could be easily grasped.

At length, he stole his opportunity to survey the map, scrutinizing every possible route. He even went so far as to contemplate a passage labelled *Forbidden Pass*. Problem was, it was the swiftest path. It was impossible for him not to consider it. Yet, there was this baggage with him. Glancing up, he found her attention absorbed by the shimmering brook. She must be bored. Responding to a puzzling spasm of pity, he plopped down beside her.

"Take the other end of this," he directed with map in hand. "You see this trail? That is where we sit. We should be relatively safe along this course for most of the way. But this bend is where the tribe suggests we turn off. I am not so sure I agree. That would cost *days.*"

It was some time before he recalled she could not answer him. When he surveyed her, he discovered her considering the name of the passage. Her eyes flicked to his. He conjectured she did not care for his suggestion.

"We can decide when we get there?" he proposed.

Her eyes cleared.

"Very well," he answered, carefully refolding the map. She struck him as a follower. He did not believe it would be difficult to convince her once they reached that juncture. "Shall we go on?"

Upon her eager nod, he aided her to her feet. He wasn't certain why he did so. It was not customary for the men of the tribes to coddle their womenfolk. Women of the clans were typically sturdy and self-assured. Rowan respected them for it. So, why was he going to extra lengths for this bit of a thing? It was as if the frailty of his boyhood was rearing its ugly head again. He must not fall prey to the past. His upbringing had taught him better.

He proceeded to cast glances over his shoulder to be certain they were not followed. They would soon come upon the Tribe of Blooms. Their clans had not been at peace for very long. One never knew what mischief other tribes might be up to when it came to the recompense. Though they had been urged to spend their first night with the village, Rowan felt it was best not to trust them too far.

Jaela grasped his wrist, instantly halting him. He opened his mouth to question her when he heard it, too. They were being tailed. His eyes darted to her face. He noted how the hand on his wrist trembled like a startled bird. Her large eyes were wide with panic.

With a wink, he raised his bow as if to scorn whomever dared follow them. He knew he could best anyone he liked with a single arrow. Just give him a target. Raising a finger for silence, he bade her remain where she was. She released him with an uncertain smile.

Stealthily, he picked his way through the forest. He was made for situations like this. With reliable ears and a silent tread, he effortlessly judged the position of their adversary. After making a wide ring in order to take their follower by surprise, he pointed the tip of his arrow into the back of a hooded figure.

"Drop your weapons," he ordered.

With a squeal, none other than Briar dropped her bow and twirled to face him. "For the heavens above, you would not shoot your own kin?!"

Rowan promptly lowered his arrow as a storm brewed over his head. "What are you *doing* here, Briar? And where *were* you this morning?"

After reaching for her fallen weapon, she relaxed into her customary wide-legged stance. "Been waiting for you near that brook. It certainly took you long enough to arrive. How much time do you think there is before the Celestial Spectacle?"

Rowan shook his head. "I am missing something here. Why would you wish to say goodbye to me *here?*"

She raised an amused brow. "I am coming along, you silly brute."

The brother blinked back at her. "Y-you cannot do that. Father would kill us! They will not know what has become of you."

"I left a note under Mother's pillow," she answered easily.

"But... you were not selected!"

"Who *cares?* I do not see what it can hurt to have another along. Only reason they do not send more is because of how perilous the Nethers is. But I *long* for an adventure. Besides, you need me, Ro. Jaela is not going to do you much good. Admit it. Once you have had a moment to digest it, you will be glad I came."

Rowan shook his head. It was true her company was desirable, even if she did possess the tread of a bear. But putting his sister in harm's way was no pleasure excursion. Though he would never admit it, he had always been relieved when she was not selected as champion. She was far too eager to meet danger. And she was fortunate she had no cause for harboring fear. He was of no mind to see that altered.

"No, Briar. I am not volunteering to watch your back on top of hers."

Briar raised a brow at him, crossing her arms in the process. "I would like to see you *try* to send me back. First available chance, I would come racing after you. I do not care how qualified you are. I am not leaving you on your own."

Rowan's mind raced through his options. He was uncertain there was anything to be done. Briar's resolves were out of his hands. When she determined to have her way, she got it.

A twig snapped as Jaela tiptoed into the expanse. She peered questioningly from one to the other.

Rubbing at the back of his neck, Rowan turned to her with helplessness. "Er, Jaela… it seems Briar has a hankering to encounter the very abyss of the Nethers itself. You mind?"

Her brows flew to her hairline as she considered Briar's presence. Rowan would have given much to become acquainted with the path her considerations took before she finally nodded with just the hint of a smirk. Whatever her reasons, she liked this turn of events. He was almost sure it was for his sake. She had grasped his agitation and was pleased his sister had not forsaken him. For that matter, so was he.

"Briar," he voiced with a sigh. "It seems the lady favors your petition. You may come."

Briar flashed a grin. "As if *either* of you was going to manage leaving me behind without tying me up and leaving me for wolf bait."

CHAPTER 7

JAELA'S HEAD SPUN OVER the term "lady" used in reference to herself. Unbeknownst to Rowan, she cast a searching look his way. What was there about him that made him treat her as more human than most, that caused him to inquire of her about their route or whether Briar should be permitted to enlist in their exploit? He was the shining star of Deerskin. He had no pretext to see her as anything more than the wild thing who could not speak aright. For years, he had avoided her. But when forced into her presence, he made her feel like an equal. It was both discomfiting and rather wonderful.

As they continued along the path, the siblings argued over whether Briar's actions had been appropriate. The addition of the sister was certainly going to make their travels more diverting. Rowan had someone to converse with and she could listen on. However, she understood he would lean on the stronger girl over herself. She had appreciated him inquiring of her. But she knew she was no real company. Now, she had but to shadow the young warriors and trust they could take care of each other. As for her, she had HS... so she hoped.

That *was* a question. He had sent her off on this dangerous passage for a purpose, but her presence was utterly futile now. He would have done better to select the siblings in the first place. So, what was her place? And how would she manage to keep herself from becoming a burden to these capable people should danger ensue?

HS, she whispered in her mind, recalling how he had spoken into hers the evening of the choosing. Surely, if he were nearby in some unseen way, he would answer. According to his promise, he was to be watching out for her. But no response followed. Warily eyeing the other sojourners, she whispered his name. But the light of her flame managed to catch Briar's attention.

"Sorry, Jaela," she remarked. "I suppose you are not looking forward to being stuck in the middle of brother and sister arguments the whole way. Come on, Ro. We are bound to drive the girl nutty with you chastising me nonstop. Let us play a game of seek-find. I will begin. I have spotted something red."

Jaela caught sight of a red bird some way ahead, but how she was meant to communicate this was beyond her. The siblings did not heed her difficulty as they resumed their game—Rowan with irritation, Briar without a care.

Ergo, Jaela's mind was left to its own devices once again. How could HS protect her if he wasn't here? Had he called her out only to desert her? She began to seriously consider entrusting these two with the quest and returning home. Her people already scorned her. Not much would change.

Then again, she recalled the reason she had assented to HS's request. He had wanted *her*. And she loved him. She could not deny him. And what did she care if she passed away in pursuit of his purposes? What was there to live for in this world for an all but unloved girl? With this cheerful view, the afternoon wiled away.

Just before sunset, they reached the outskirts of the Tribe of Blooms. It was customary for friendly tribes to host traveling champions at this time of year. Jaela waited to see what the siblings would decide.

"You two remain here..." Rowan directed meditatively, "while I meet with their leader."

"Why would we do that?" Briar questioned.

"I want to make certain we can trust these people before we tuck ourselves into their village for the night."

"Riiight," Briar murmured doubtfully. "So, when they prove unsafe, we can just stop in and rescue you on our way out? Let us face this as a band. Safety in numbers and all that. We might arm Jaela with a dagger to make her appear a little more formidable."

Rowan's face clouded with disapproval, but he inevitably consented. Jaela perceived he was fearful for his sister's safety. She had hoped having the adept Briar along would prove a comfort. It only seemed to increase his burden. Apparently, Jaela had more faith in his sister than he did. She'd *like* to see someone provoke the girl's fury. It would not end well for them.

Briar proceeded to strap a dagger belt about Jaela's waist and offer tutelage in how to tread like a hunter. Jaela doubted her slight attributes could pull it off, but Briar did not seem altogether dissatisfied with the result.

"You will do," she assured.

Jaela couldn't help being pleased, even if it was over something as trivial as walking. If there was anything she could do, it was walk. *Maiden of talent, folks,* she thought mirthfully. A soft chuckle escaped her that sent up a wisp of flame. Briar eyed her sidelong but said nothing. Rowan was too focused on their surroundings.

With something like a choke, Jaela stopped short. The siblings hesitated briefly before resuming their course. Jaela remained captive to the enthralling fragrance that permeated the breeze. *Roses.* This was the Tribe of Blooms, after all.

It was as she rejoined the siblings that she caught her first sight of the alluring garden. Like nature's tapestry, numerous buds bobbed in copious hues upon shrubs and vines. The trees in this area were sparse, allowing generous golden rays from a departing sun to illuminate the oasis.

In hushed wonder, the three ambled among the flora. It wasn't until they reached the final hedges that Jaela stopped short again. Here danced a unique sampling of dark crimson blooms that boasted smoldering shadows in contrast to glowing, ember-like facets. They seared the atmosphere with a spicy aroma, like apples stewed with cinnamon. Jaela yearned to exclaim over them, but she dared not. It exasperated her that those who *could* do so chose merely to exit the garden.

Jaela couldn't resist pressing her nose deep into the fullest bud, imbuing her lungs with its perfume. It would have been impossible for her to describe the sensation that followed, even in an ordinary tongue. Tenderly, she pressed her cheek to the cool petals. Her soul ached for splendor like this. Could such ecstasies be why HS had pried her from her mother's skirt-tails and into the wide-open world? Could there be more enchanting experiences like this to come?

"You like my blooms, do ya?" the voice of an elder woman inquired from the other side of the shrubbery.

Jaela bounced to face her intruder, inadvertently carving her hand across one of the thorny branches. Burning accompanied the red that emerged from her skin. How could such charming, delicate things prove so hazardous?

"Now, I've gone and done it!" the woman mused as she took immediate possession of the bleeding hand. "You'll have to stand still a mite while I apply my salve. A prick from this bush'll send a fire straight up yer arm. Akin to flame, them shrubs be. Developed 'em myself, with the aid of a friend, as a defensive procedure. But I canna tell ya how many innocents is been wounded. Twas a foolish notion, I warrant. But they're too lovely to undo, so I've made my bed, ya see."

She directed a wrinkly grin into the face of the girl who stood frozen and helpless for what to do. She had lost track of her companions and was now alone with a stranger from another tribe. But she was powerless against the burning that ensued as foreboded.

"I reckon yer from Deerskin, ain't ya?" the woman commented as she finished applying the salve.

Jaela's eyes flew to the woman's face. How could she know?

"Yer friends' clothes, girly," she explained over the length of bandage she unwound. "Them deerskins is a dead giveaway. Most folks wears *bear*, you know"

Jaela glanced down at her own garment in perplexity.

"And yer getup is of Evangeline the Weaver, that's clear. I own a piece of hers myself. Tiz old but holds well. Don't know how the woman does it. Especially the spinning of them tiny fibers. Tiz a mystery what them river peoples used to manage. Still, they passed on the secrets of the roses to us and we've kept on, you see."

Having completed her work, the woman's eyes flashed to Jaela's in question. "Ah... I haven't offered my name, have I? Old Willow, they call me. Who might you be?"

Jaela's lips parted. It had been so long since anyone had spoken to her and expected an answer that she almost offered one. Yet, the flame that would inevitably follow never failed to produce terror. She pointed to her mouth to convey her inability to speak when Rowan appeared in breathlessness at her side.

"For *heavens*, Jaela, I thought something had happened to you," he scolded. "We have already met the tribe leader and been granted a place for rest. Will you not come along?" With a curt nod at Old Willow, he turned his back on them, clearly expecting Jaela to obey.

Sending the elder a generous nod of farewell, Jaela raced after Rowan. Reaching his side, she noted his resolute march. Suddenly, he halted to face her.

"You cannot be doing things like that. Something might really happen next time and I might not assume you are in need of help."

Jaela offered a sorrowful expression. She so valued the regard he had displayed for her thus far and was of no mind to lose it. It hurt her that she had displeased him. Even so, she had not intended to cause a problem. How could she help it in future?

Releasing a long breath, he confessed, "You have every right to do as you please, Jaela. I just want to make certain you are safe… All right?"

The frank way his eyes shone revealed he truly had been anxious. This produced a whole new view of him. No one but Evangeline considered her wellbeing. Nor had this young man ever struck her as the mother-hen sort. But there was something parental about him now. It was as if she was his responsibility, as if she actually mattered in the scheme of things.

With a hearty nod, she met his gaze, exuding all the promise she could into it.

Unexpectedly, a humbled smirk flashed across his face. "Thanks," he answered before continuing on.

Jaela was surprised by the sensation that followed. Her interactions with the esteemed lad felt something akin with companionship. He read her with ease, worried after her wellbeing, validated her humanity. Could this be the dawning of her first real friendship? Try as she might to squelch the hope, she couldn't help herself.

"So, you are in one piece, are you?" Briar observed when they entered a rose-covered dwelling. "I assured Rowan of as much, but he *would* go after you."

Rowan's eyes flicked to Jaela's as he spoke, "Observe her hand and you will find she was not entirely out of danger."

Briar's gaze flew to the bandage. "Get caught in a rosebush?"

With a mortified shrug, Jaela nodded her admission.

"Well, remain mindful," Briar advised. "The place is *crawling* with them. Cannot see how they expect me to breathe, let alone sleep." She swatted a hand before her face as if to wave off the fragrance. Eyeing the fresh bouquet on the table, she plucked it up and tossed it out the nearest window. "Perhaps that will get me through."

Jaela's heart whimpered with affrontery at the same time Rowan spoke, "You should not have done that, Briar. It is an insult. These people as near as worship their roses. And I do not think they smell so bad."

"Well, you *would* say that. They smell like your silly Caspa."

Jaela shot a glance at the young man she was growing to like. Could he be betrothed to *Caspa,* of all people? The very one who had teased and bullied her all through the years? She didn't seem a fitting companion for him.

"*My* Caspa?" he growled. "I told you I have no mind to be tied down."

"Oh, *right*. You have places to see, honors to win. But in the end, Caspa is too pretty not to get her way."

Jaela shuddered as she perused what her mother had packed, absently wondering if it was any use attempting to dress well for evening meal. Meanwhile, she couldn't help pitying the man who joined with her fiend. But it was really none of her affair. She simply must not form an attachment to one who would eventually be within Caspa's clutches. He likely had no interest in befriending her anyway.

CHAPTER 8

JAELA WAS UNEXPECTEDLY EAGER for her first evening meal away from home. Since none knew her as the fire-breathing wild thing, she could go about as if she were anyone... at least, anyone who could not speak. Hopefully, that was all her companions would intimate. After all, it didn't make them look well to be seen with her for what she actually was.

Torches lit the well-trodden paths of Blooms. Their flames seemed only to augment the aroma of the blossoms that climbed the dwellings. Briar coughed now and then as if she truly could not bear their fragrance. This served as amusement for both Rowan and Jaela, who eyed one another sidelong with her every fit.

"It is not funny, you two!" Briar retorted when they relented to soft chuckles. "How am I supposed to *eat* tonight?" She swatted the air. "Makes me sick to my stomach... *Blech.*"

They entered a dining area similar to that of Deerskin. The only real variance were the stone columns on each corner of the expanse from between which rose garlands were suspended.

Briar froze to scowl up at them, to which Rowan and Jaela were forced to bite their cheeks.

Uncertain of where to seat themselves, they stood awkwardly some time before a thin fellow near their age approached. "You are in for quite an evening," he said congenially, "but I do not suppose it is not anything you have not already seen, seeing as you are champions yourselves."

Rowan nodded. "We were informed this is the evening of your Selection Ceremony. We look forward to witnessing it."

"Should be interesting. You will be seated with me, will you not?"

Jaela discovered his eyes on her. Uncomfortably, she drew behind Briar. Had the siblings apprised these people of her inadequacies? Or was it her appearance? She had obeyed her mother in running a comb through her hair. Her clothes were freshly woven—an order Evangeline had designed for another but felt Jaela now required.

As the four started for their seats, Briar cast Jaela a wink over her shoulder. Was she teasing her for having already begun to attract unwanted attention? A knot twisted in her stomach as her prior excitement gave way to dread. Would things never be different?

Jaela took a seat beside Briar, eyes fixed on the bonfire. She sensed some confusion as Rowan nearly appropriated the seat beside her but ended by forfeiting it to their host. Jaela shivered as she questioned whether their new acquaintance had been assigned to keep watch of her.

"What was it like?" the stranger asked without warning. "Your selection?"

Jaela awaited an answer from one of the siblings when Briar nudged her. Jaela's eyes darted to hers and then to the lad's. His eyes were on her again. As her own eyes bulged, she searched for what to do when Briar spoke up.

"This is Jaela, daughter of Krin the Honorable and Evangeline the Weaver. She cannot speak."

"Ah," he replied with the momentary drooping of his features. When his gaze returned to her, he spoke with a proffered hand, "I am Jethro. I did not see you with the others when they arrived."

Jaela eyed his hand before finally taking it into her own for a moment and swiftly returning hers to the security of her lap.

"She admires your roses," Briar shared with a hardy effort to cover her own disdain for them.

"*Aaah,*" he replied, clearly pleased. "And which were your favorite, Jaela? The yellows? Pinks?"

Jaela shook her head at each of these. She knew without contemplation which she preferred.

"Not the flaming crimsons?" he inquired with a wry grin.

Jaela's eyes lit up as she nodded.

The fellow's brows rose as his eyes darted to the fire. If he had not already been put off, he was now, though she couldn't tell why. Perhaps normal girls didn't admire plants whose thorns were like poison. But Jaela was merely relieved to ascertain her secret was not known to this tribe. She cast a thankful gaze to the starry sky above, feeling at her ease once again.

Jethro clucked. "Dangerous beasts, those blooms." Considering her profile some moments, he added, "I am glad you like them. They are my grandmother's innovation."

Jaela's eyes flew to his. She wished she could intimate that she had met the woman. After a moment, inspiration dawned. She pointed to her bandaged hand.

His eyes widened first with confusion, then surprise. "You have met her? *Oh,* I apologize for the circumstances..." He gestured to the bandage.

A near duplicate of Jethro quietly seated himself before the bonfire. Much like his lookalike, he was tall and lanky, but he did not raise his gaze to his neighbors so easily as Jethro.

"This is Farrow," Jethro introduced with a pat to the lad's back, "my brother."

Jaela couldn't help presuming him a twin. She wished Briar would ask.

"Farrow, meet our visitors from Deerskin."

Farrow offered the slightest eye-contact, along with a nod, before returning his attention to the fire. Jaela decided he was either very shy or very serious. Perhaps both. He glanced up once more to catch her staring.

Averting her gaze, she was rescued by the appearance of a server bearing a platter of skewered fish. While the group busied themselves with roasting, Jaela surveyed the remainder of the company at their fire with surprise. When had all the young ladies arrived? Watching them vie for Rowan's attention, she ascertained their purpose. And she could not blame them. Not only was he recognized as the son of his revered father among many of the clans, he was tall, strapping and possessed a ready smile. Furthermore, he was a chosen champion for this annum's recompense. Should he return, he would be at least something of a hero. She supposed there would be many young women hoping he might return for them.

With a mouth full, Jethro questioned, "So, how did your tribe end up with *three* champions?"

Briar shook her head. "These two were selected. I am tagging along."

"Is that allowed?"

She shrugged. "I never asked."

With a smirk that revealed his appreciation of her rogue act, he turned once again to Jaela. "How do you care for the fish?"

Jaela nodded her appreciation. If she didn't know any better, she would conjecture it was stuffed with rose petals. By the way Briar kept tossing covert pieces into the fire, she established this was correct.

As another server passed with skewers wrapped in bread dough, Jethro took the liberty of fetching one for her along with his own. Jaela contemplated this attention while she watched him roast their food. Was this the kind of behavior shown to normal girls? Unconsciously, her eyes flew to Briar, who answered her with a telling smirk.

Jaela felt her face flush. It couldn't be true. No one had ever found her appealing. How could one take interest in someone who could not speak? Yet, Jethro persisted in showing her special consideration throughout the remainder of the meal.

To her astonishment, she grew accustomed rather quickly. It was enjoyable passing for an ordinary girl to a congenial young man. She might never have this chance again. Yet, she questioned his motivation. Was she perhaps... *fair* to look upon when she was made neat? Certainly, she could not possess anything like her mother's beauty. But maybe one did not have to appear like someone formerly of the River's Way in order to be comely enough to be noticed. It was a complete revelation to her, this notion that she might not be repulsive.

At the close of the meal, a woman whom Jaela took to be the tribe leader announced the typical Selection Ceremony oration. Jaela tuned out as she stole pieces from the fluffy fruit of the final course. It was some time before she realized something was wrong. Looking up in search of a cause for the murmurs among the populace, she discovered they were unable to light their ceremonial fire. They used the same wood as the remainder of the clans, but she ascertained they had chosen their pieces poorly.

"That does not bode well," Briar murmured as if washing her hands of it.

Rowan nudged her. "It will take many days for them to fetch new wood from beside the River Lifespring. Their champions will have less time in which to reach the Nethers with their recompense."

Jaela's concern was cut short by a rushing resonance in her ears. She closed her eyes, willing it away. This was one of her impulses—a side-effect that had accompanied her strange language. She arose, hoping to get away before it had its way with her. She had not taken two steps when Briar grasped her garment.

"What is the matter?" she questioned with concern.

Jaela shook her head, flushing as Jethro's eyes searched her in turn. She felt herself tear from Briar's grasp. Her feet strode to the center of the fires until she was before the ceremonial tinder. Squatting down, she stole one long breath and then blew. Fire in the hues of a ceremonial flame streamed from her lips until the wood blazed into a seething inferno. Its heat cast her back upon the ground.

All was silent but the crackling of the wood. Jaela's eyes watered as she surveyed the flames. She was known to perform peculiar acts among her own people but never before *strangers*. Her odds of passing as normal were vanished. News of her strangeness would spread. She was marked... again.

Scrambling to her feet, she caught glimpses of astonished faces. She kept her eyes on the turf as she raced from the expanse and down the path until she reached their cabin. Flinging the door closed behind her, she fell upon her bedroll on the floor, relenting to sobs.

She knew it would not have been half so humiliating if she had not allowed herself to enjoy Jethro's attention. She had almost begun to feel herself the carefree young woman he had thought her, one in whom someone might actually take an interest. She had been a fool to entertain herself so childishly. That could never be her lot.

She awoke sometime later to Briar's animated articulations as she stalked into the cabin. She proceeded to light the nearest candles before taking a seat at the table. Rowan's admonishing hush reached Jaela's ears as she sensed him point in her direction.

"Jaela, wake up!" Briar exclaimed in response. "You must hear this."

It was some moments before Jaela's curiosity got the better of her. She opened her eyes in time to catch Rowan gesturing for Briar to let her sleep. It was a generous thought but too late.

She sat up, groggily pushing the tendrils from her face. Her eyes searched Briar as if to say, "Go on."

Briar surprised her by rising from her chair to sit upon the end of Jaela's bedroll.

"You will *never* guess what happened."

Jaela blinked back. Hadn't the horrific already taken place when she had lit the ceremonial fire with her breath?

"I was chosen as a champion for the Tribe of Blooms."

Jaela blinked back, rubbing the sleep from her eyes. She could not have heard aright. Champions were chosen from *within* the tribe on behalf of the tribe. Surely, it was reckless to entrust the recompense to any other.

"Yes, *really*," Briar answered with a laugh. "Here, I thought I was defying our customs and now I have been *legitimately* selected to carry a recompense for some tribe I do not care two hoots about! But... I have a *chance*... to prove myself rightfully."

Before Jaela knew what she was about, she had grasped Briar's elbows with excitement. She shook her lightly as if to shout, *"Hurrah!"* Perhaps only those in the cabin had any inkling of what this meant to the younger child of Bowan the Champion.

Briar giggled, grasping Jaela in the same manner. *"See,* Rowan," she called. "Jaela understands. This is the chance of a lifetime!"

"They will not allow it, Briar," he answered soberly from where he sat at the table. "Entrusting their salvation to the citizen of another clan. They will think—" He stopped short, eyes flashing to Jaela before darting away. Mutely, he stood and began to unpack his bedroll.

"What?" Briar pressed, all delight absent from her voice. "You think..." Her eyes met Jaela's. "You think they will suppose she rigged the fire somehow?"

He did not speak, which was all the answer required.

The wind in Jaela's sails died out as the shame of what she had involuntarily done returned full force. Could her actions cost Briar this opportunity?

Briar eyed her in question some moments before, "Do not think I am blaming you, Jaela. I am not. But... why did you do it—light the tinder?" She did not appear accusatory so much as perplexed. It was clear she had grasped Jaela's desire to keep her secret.

"I did not *mean*—" The explanation died on Jaela's lips as flame wisped into Briar's face. The girl did not back away. It did not burn like the fire with which Jaela had lit the ceremonial flame. Even so, it was evident how difficult it was for Briar to keep her eyes from widening over the experience.

"Leave her be," Rowan called from his bed. "Can you not see it was involuntary? It was one of those compulsions her mother says she suffers."

Briar nodded at Jaela with understanding. "Well, I do not care what they decide," she spoke slowly. Boldness gleamed in her eyes as she continued, "I was *chosen*. I will help deliver their recompense whether their other champion wants me or not." Leaping to her feet as nimbly as a deer, she stuffed herself into her bedroll.

For some time, Jaela lay awake, contemplating the events of the evening. Where exactly did her impulses derive from? How had she managed to light the wood despite its being bad? Why had Briar been selected as champion of another tribe? Was it the Creator's doing? He had chosen Jaela, after all. Perhaps he had a plan for Briar, too. Or perhaps he had taken pity on her after she had displayed such determination for the commissioning. It was legendary that the flame of another tribe had rested upon the girl. They would learn the tribe's response come morning.

CHAPTER 9

ROWAN AWOKE WITH A cloud over his head. The evening prior was the last thing anyone could have expected. He already wished his sister safe at home with their parents. Now, she had been selected as champion for Blooms. It should have been impossible. To his knowledge, nothing like it had *ever* occurred before. But he had watched the tongue of flame rest upon her head, just as it had him. Question was... *could* Jaela's lighting of the ceremonial flame have had anything to do with it? Surely, this unheard-of turn of events must look like a covert attempt to conquer the Tribe of Blooms, placing their fate into the hands of one who would not follow through.

The expected knock sounded at the door. With a growl, Briar chucked her pillow at it. Jaela bolted upright, staring at the door as if they were about to be taken from their beds and held captive. Rowan rose from his bedroll to answer.

Jethro stole a step backward as if uncertain of his welcome so early in the morning, perhaps unsure as to the trustworthiness of their presence within the village. "Er, celestial sunrise... or very nearly," he spoke as pleasantly as ever he had the evening before.

Rowan perceived the strain. "Celestial sunrise," he answered evenly, folding his arms. "What can we do for you?"

"Ah. Yes. Tribe Leader Annis sends her invitation to appear for an impromptu assembly at dawn."

"In order to discuss the events of last night," Rowan supplied.

"Uh, yes..." His eyes seemed to catch on something.

Rowan looked back to find Jaela remaking her bedroll. When he returned his gaze to Jethro, the fellow's face was white and he stole unconsciously to the side as if to escape her view.

Rowan cleared his throat. "We will be there."

Jethro nodded. "Very well. And celestial sunrise... again." Inelegantly, he turned on his heel. It was plain it was all he could do not to race from the dwelling.

Rowan closed the door and turned about to find Jaela combing her hair. This was a new habit. He was grateful for it. They were expected to appear at a number of tribes. It wouldn't do to look like unruly vagabonds. They must bring honor to Deerskin.

Rowan wasn't certain what to make of what she had accomplished the night before. Would she continue to act out in spontaneous fashion? If so... was it possible to work it to their credit? The cogs in his mind turned. Though she was a scrawny thing, it was evident Blooms now feared her. Maybe that wasn't a bad thing. It implied the group was not easy pickings.

"Hop up, Briar," he directed as he repacked his belongings. "We are invited for breakfast."

"Breakfast?" she spat, pulling aside the unruly hair that cloaked her face like a set of drapes. "I heard nothing about *breakfast*. They will just tell me to go back home. They do not want me."

Rowan observed the rare tremble in her voice. Could his ferocious little sister actually be anxious about the proceedings? "They have no right to send you home. And you have no obligation to deliver a recompense without their endorsement."

She flew from her bedroll, proceeding to roll it up with haste. "I am *going* to aid with that recompense. I was selected... something I feared would never happen. You know how much I want this."

He did, though he wished it wasn't so. "Then let us appear to best advantage—on time."

It was mere moments before the young women stood at the ready. Jaela seemed to have rushed her grooming for Briar's sake. She appeared as anxious as his sister.

"You plan to attend in the same clothes as last evening?" he asked them with a raised brow.

The two looked down at themselves, then to one another.

"We cannot change with you here, genius," Briar defended.

With a shrug, he turned for the door. "Remember, we are in a hurry. No primping."

"I thought you said we must appear at best advantage," she called as he fastened the door shut.

It wasn't long before the three appeared at the dining quarter. Rowan's supposition that this was where they held meetings had been correct. It was the same with Deerskin. Even so, he had not expected the company of elders and leaders lined on either side of what appeared like three thrones at the head of the gathering. The three were directed to traverse the path through the assemblage as if called to trial. This did not bode well.

Rowan bowed his head before the tribe leader. "Celestial sunrise, Tribe Leader Annis."

"Fair sunrise," she answered smoothly. "I trust you were comfortable in the quarters provided?"

Rowan bowed his head again. "Perfectly. We thank you."

She bowed her head in turn. "I am glad. Now, shall we dispense with the pleasantries?"

"Please," he answered with a scarcely concealed growl.

The woman smirked as if she shared his sentiment. "Clearly, we confront a dilemma. Something utterly unprecedented took place last evening. Er, that is, *two*... unprecedented happenings transpired. Firstly, was the igniting of our ceremonial fire by your fellow champion. Could you... explain her ability to perform such a feat?"

Rowan noted the murmurs of the company about them. They presumed what his own tribe had for years—Jaela must possess some kind of daemon blood. But he, of all people, felt certain this was not the case. Though even he was uncertain just who had bestowed her malady, her mother claimed it was the Creator's work. As if from above, inspiration struck.

"Are you not aware she is the daughter of Evangeline the Weaver," he asserted, "the last remaining inhabitant of the River's Way?"

Unrestrained gasps sounded. He had struck a chord. In truth, he had forgotten how impressive this was. Though Deerskin did not esteem the woman's notable heritage, this clan did.

He nodded. "Jaela of Deerskin is the only offspring from that of the river people. As her mother explains, the tongue of angels flows like righteous flame from her lips. Jaela is the only personage of such ability in all the tribes."

He felt the heat of Jaela's eyes boring into his back. What must she make of his tale? What would *Briar* make of it? Well, it mattered not. He felt himself weaving as skillfully as Evangeline herself.

"I apologize," Tribe Leader Annis began tentatively. "We were not aware there *were* any offspring of the River's Way." She nodded to Jaela as if to dignify her position. "We are... grateful for your contribution to our Selection Ceremony." It was clear this transition from suspicion to reverence was an uncertain shift for the leader.

"You mentioned a second matter?" Rowan questioned before the woman saw fit to alter the course he had constructed.

Annis nodded. "It is utterly unheard of that a young person from an outside clan be selected as champion. Considering it was your champion who blew the flame into being, there were misgivings as to whether it was some prearranged conjuring..."

Rowan bowed as if to convey his understanding. "We feared it may be taken thus. But... who can dispute the inclinations of angels?" Was comparing Jaela to the creatures of legend going too far?

As appeased chuckles rumbled through the gathering, Tribe Leader Annis raised a brow. "I would like to hear from the lady in question herself."

Rowan grasped for a means of persuading this company as to the "wonder" of Jaela's inability to speak their language. "Er, Jaela of Deerskin—"

Tribe Leader Annis shook her head. "I meant this daughter of Bowan the Champion—the one called Briar, I believe." Her gaze went beyond him. "What have you to say concerning your selection, young woman?"

With a curious blend of boldness and unprecedented meekness, Briar stepped around Rowan. Offering a low bow to the tribe leader, she began, "Every year since I became of age for the Selection Ceremony, I have yearned to be chosen to deliver our recompense. I... regret to admit that, when I was not selected this annum, I, er, selected myself for the expedition."

Rumblings of disapproval resounded.

Rowan made ready to step in with swift tongue when she continued, "I consider it a higher honor than I could have imagined that I have been selected to deliver the recompense for *this* tribe. I assure you that I will do *everything* in my power to see it swiftly performed... should you grant your approval."

Annis released a long breath as she considered Briar for some moments. She turned first to the elder on her left and then her right for private conference. Rowan could not decide whether he hoped for or against their sanction. But in the end, Briar was intent upon making the journey. She may as well gain all the glory she could from it.

"Farrow of Blooms," the tribe leader called in conclusion of their briefing.

In answer, the fellow who had been selected as champion along with Briar stepped from the crowd. Rowan was struck by how similarly he appeared to his brother, Jethro.

"Are you willing to carry the recompense alongside Briar of Deerskin, daughter of Bowan the Champion?"

For some moments, Farrow neglected to speak. Finally, he cleared his throat. "It would be an honor to carry the recompense with whomever the Creator of fire deems."

Annis nodded as if pleased with her citizen. To the surprise of all, however, she called, "Elaine of Blooms, are you present?"

Rowan found himself struck dumb by the sight of the tall, golden-haired maiden who stepped forward.

"You have volunteered to accompany Farrow in place of Briar," Tribe Leader Annis continued. "Are you further willing to accompany them *both* as a reserve resident champion on behalf of Blooms?"

Rowan watched Briar's hands tighten into fists as the company cheered this decision. She considered the proposition an insult. But a volunteer to travel into the Nethers was a rarity. He had thought Briar the only such lunatic. If all went as the tribe leader proposed, Rowan was in for quite a handful.

Elaine nodded without hesitation. "It would be my honor, Tribe Leader."

Tribe Leader Annis was appeased. She gestured for the two young villagers of Blooms to join those of Deerskin. Once the five were aligned according to her direction, she bid them turn and face the assembly.

"Tribe of Blooms," she announced, "for perhaps the first time in the history of the recompense, here stands a joint effort to present the recompenses of two allied tribes before the end of the Celestial Spectacle. Please join me in bidding them farewell and celestial fortunes in the commissioning they must precipitously undertake."

Rowan's eyes narrowed as the company stomped their appreciation. This was not how things were supposed to have gone. He wasn't certain he had it in him to trust members of another tribe for the whole of a journey, especially when they were sending a spare champion. What if they should see fit to bring about the demise of Deerskin, just as they had conjectured had been plotted against them? He would have to be on double lookout, always wondering if enemies had been planted right into their midst. Even so, Briar had been chosen and accepted. There was no denying that. They must all endure the consequences.

CHAPTER 10

JAELA REELED AS THEY departed from the dining area. Not only had they just been intimately entangled with the Tribe of Blooms for the remainder of their quest, Rowan had painted her as an unparalleled heroine. Could he truly believe the things he had spoken? How she wished he had spouted such things among their own. It would have altered her whole existence. But now he had made such claims before Blooms, it could not be unsaid. Word would spread. Would it be to her benefit or ill? Perhaps, in the end, it mattered little. It was but one journey. Then again, it had become an unprecedented one—the uniting of two tribes, their destinies interwoven.

They were told breakfast would be served in their cabin while Farrow and Elaine prepared for the venture. They would depart as soon as possible. No one wanted to chance their champions appearing late with a recompense. The three ate around their table in silence, mulling over the events that lay behind and before.

Finally, Briar's eyes pierced each of them in turn. "So... Jaela's next door to an angel, huh?"

Jaela blinked. This wasn't the route she had expected the girl's thoughts to take. She had just been established as the champion she longed to be. Surely, that must be foremost in her mind.

Rowan's glance to Jaela was swift before it returned to his food. He shrugged. "It is what her mother always maintained. What else was there to say? Any other explanation is pure conjecture. And she *is* a descendant of the river people."

Briar eyed Jaela in contemplation, as if considering these new concepts. "How long have you thought this way?" she asked him.

Jaela wished she could speak up. It was difficult being discussed without the ability to enter her own questions.

Rowan shrugged again. "Always, I suppose. Why should I not think so?"

Jaela took her turn at examining Rowan. He really did see her differently than others. This was no small matter to one who had lived as she. A peculiar sweeping of her heart took place every time she thought of it. Or was it her stomach?

Taking her off her guard, his eyes returned to her in open contemplation. She was certain he wished to say something. Why did he appear so... shamefaced?

A knock jolted them. At Briar's call, Jethro appeared for the second time. He shuffled in with a similar discomfiture as the first instance, but this time he did not avoid Jaela's gaze. His expression was questioning. Though her reputation had been salvaged, he did not know what to make of her. She remained an enigma.

"They are ready for you in the garden," he announced, "and have almost concluded their farewells."

Rowan nodded. "Our thanks, Jethro. Am I right in thinking Farrow your twin?"

He nodded.

"Really?" Briar questioned. "He seems so..."

"Serious?" he suggested. "We are quite different. Still, we have always been close."

"Was it difficult to see him selected over yourself?" Briar asked with understanding.

His eyes flicked to Jaela before returning to Briar. "Yes."

With a bow, he made his exit.

Briar chuckled. "Jaela, my friend, I would say you have yourself a love interest."

Jaela scowled. *Some* love interest—afraid of her one moment, making hesitant puppy eyes the next. Even so, it made her blush. Perhaps he wasn't a faultless admirer, but he was her first. He had revealed she was not altogether disagreeable to look upon. She would not soon forget it. Having only just departed from her village, her world was already altered by this finding alone.

They had just reached the flaming blossoms when Old Willow stepped into Jaela's path. Since the others were before her, she had no way of alerting them that she must stop a moment.

"Pardon me, dearie," the elder began. "I just wanted to wish ya luck in yer journey. And to say I'll be prayin' after ya, that all goes well."

Jaela felt the corners of her eyes crinkle in gratefulness. This was a rare sentiment, especially for someone like herself.

"I'd heard of ya," Old Willow explained, "the little 'wild thing,' so they call ya."

Jaela felt her countenance drop by several degrees.

"But I'd not realized just what ya were," the woman went on. "A *firetongue.*" She bowed her head. "It is an honor to meet one of such distinction within the Creator's circle."

Jaela's spirit bounded. That was what Elder Si had called her. What did these elders know that she did not? How could she provoke the woman to explain? She reached for Willow's hand, gripping it like a lifeline. Not knowing what else to do, she put out her tongue and pointed to it with all the question she could muster into her eyes.

Old Willow hesitated. "Y-you don't *know* what ya are?" she asked. "Aye, and neither did my grandsons when I told 'em last night. You young one's wouldn't know. Not even yer own parents, I grant. The firetongues is an all but forgotten clan—an offshoot from those of the River's Way. You've heard tell of Evangeline the Weaver, ain't ya?"

Jaela nodded exuberantly, pointing to her heart.

Old Willow's eyes narrowed with consternation before clearing. "Yer *hers,* are ya? I plumb fergot my grandsons' mention of it. Well, I suppose that explains it. Though I don't see how

Evangeline couldn't have knowed of yer kind. She's a *good* many years of age, ain't she? But then... I believe even her kind weren't certain what to make of the firetongues. They abandoned the river people, after all, and became nomads. They say the river folk writ them off fer it.

"Now, I suppose yer wonderin' why I should know so much. You see, I met myself a firetongue once. Was the one what taught me to make the flaming blooms what you so admire. But he did a lot more n' that fer me. He *healed* me. I was a cripple all my life, and a bitter one. When his fire coursed through me like what yers done last night, I tell ya I were healed body and soul."

She considered Jaela some moments before, "But I reckon you be wantin' to know what made the firetongues what they was. That fellow told me all about it. They was a particular group among those of the River's Way who especially sought after the very presence of the Creator, what they called the Great One. They done so day and night, night and day—in shifts, ya might say. Can't say what made 'em so ardent. They just *wanted* him like he was life an' breath.

"One day, it seems, when they was all gathered together, a formidable wind done whooshed through the forest. They feared it a powerful storm and thought to take shelter before these fiery tongues come down from on-high to rest upon their heads—much like what we see at the Selection Ceremonies, I reckon. From that point on, they displayed curious abilities, like what you done last night.

"Now, far as I know, all them firetongues is died off. I can't say why a new one has arisen, but I suppose it be for unusual purposes." She planted fists on her hips while she surveyed Jaela, as if searching for answers. Softly, she finished, "I look forward to hearing tales of who ya prove to be one of these days."

Jaela felt chills flush through her form. It was incredible to think this woman believed *she* had a purpose, just like HS had claimed. She now wondered if everything might have been different if she had possessed the courage to step from her village years ago. Would she have encountered those like Old Willow, who made her feel like a blessed enigma?

"I wonder..." Willow spoke hesitantly. "Perhaps tiz rude to ask, but... could I hear ya—hear yer fire-language? I ain't experienced it since I knowed that other fellow so many years back. It was a pleasing sound, I recall. Made the hairs of my arms stand right up on end while I watched my crippled legs grow strong and right again."

Jaela took a step back. No one save her mother had ever wished to hear her speak, nor actually *requested* she do so. Her voice, with its fearsome flame, was something to be abhorred. She spoke only to Evangeline and HS. How would this woman respond to her utterance? She wasn't certain she dared do as entreated.

Seeing her hesitation, Old Willow pressed, "Couldn't you answer me a question in yer tongue?"

Jaela's head bobbed to the side while she considered this. She found she longed to speak as the woman desired. She might never be asked again.

"I wonder, could ya answer me how many years I got left on Kaern? Been feelin' my age for a time now... Might be good to know."

Jaela squinted. How could she know what the woman's remaining years were? "I cannot say," she replied without thinking.

The flame that arose from her imperceptible words swirled about Old Willow's head. With wide eyes, they watched as it hastened round and round her form before vanishing into thin air at her feet. When Jaela returned her gaze to the woman's face, she stole another step back. It simply could not be!

"*My*, that were warm and satisfyin'," Old Willow sighed. "Wasn't expectin' it, but I can't say I regret it. Feel myself fresher somehow." She lifted a leg and then another, adding a little jig to her movements.

All Jaela could do was stare back. Old Willow appeared a good twenty or so years younger. Releasing an awed breath, her typical flame was emitted—nothing like what had just occurred. Why were her strange impulses ensuing more often since her departure from Deerskin?

"Well, twas a beautiful sound and a rewardin' sight. I thank ya fer that."

Old Willow did not seem to comprehend what had transpired. Jaela wondered how she would feel when she did, if her people would even recognize her. Either way, Jaela must avoid being caught in another of her episodes. She waved a swift hand in farewell and turned on her heel, marching in the direction the others had gone.

"Here you are, slowpoke," Briar greeted at sight of her. "They have finished their sendoff observances. We were just about to leave when Rowan pointed out you were missing. I think he would have raced back for you if he were not so detained."

She pointed out where her brother stood surrounded by the young women of the clan. Though he clearly enjoyed it, it was evident he was working himself from the group. He cast an anxious glance at the garden. Briar called to him, pointing to where Jaela stood beside her. With a frustrated sigh, he widened his eyes at Jaela before restoring his attention to his admirers.

"And he thinks he is going to get away with remaining single for the next ten years," Briar commented with mirth. "As if they will let him."

Jaela only wished Rowan would finish up so they could be on their way. She desperately hoped to avoid having to answer for what she had done to Old Willow. She had never accomplished anything quite like it and that frightened her. She dreaded to think what might happen the next time she opened her mouth.

CHAPTER 11

"I THOUGHT WE AGREED you would stick close?" Rowan reminded Jaela as the party departed from Blooms.

She peered up with a remorseful expression. It was apparent she wished to explain but had no way of knowing he would understand if she did. They had spent but a day together and already the contrition of his lie was catching up with him.

Her eyes went wide as she watched him watch her. Something of his thoughts had played across his face, provoking her curiosity. Well, he was no more interested in conveying his secret now as in the years prior.

"I understand," he answered softly instead. "Something came up. I will try to keep a better lookout."

She blinked back at him in confusion. He supposed she wondered why he troubled to keep such a watch. There were a number of reasons. Firstly, it would look well to return with his comrades intact. Secondly, he was experiencing a peculiar protectiveness for the two of his clan. It was a facet he never realized he suffered. He simply could not bear the thought of them coming to harm. As the strongest member of their expedition, it fell to him to see none did. This might prove difficult in the presence of an external clan. He must determine what kind of danger they might pose.

With a quick pat to Jaela's back, he left her behind in order to acquaint himself with them. Like a girl after his own heart, Briar was already doing likewise with Elaine. But he preferred his own judgement.

Offering a hand to the Blooms girl, he greeted, "Rowan of Deerskin."

She accepted it but replied nonchalantly, "Your name is no surprise to me."

He lifted his brows in question.

"You were the name on every girl's tongue this morning. And everyone knows of your father. I must say you are not quite what I expected."

He nearly choked. "What were you expecting?"

She considered a moment. "I heard the way you defended your fellow champion at the sunrise meeting. I would have supposed you too lofty to bother."

"Well," he began, clearing his throat in search of how to respond. He did not wish to appear too close with someone like Jaela. But it also suited him to keep up the façade that she was something special. "She is the offspring of the river people, after all."

"I have heard of her. Your people call her a possessor of daemon blood." She eyed him sidelong.

"My people do not know of what they speak," he barked.

A slow grin overspread her face. "See what I mean? I expected you to toss her under the deer's hooves, if you catch my meaning."

Rowan was not sure what to make of this. He was accustomed to blatant flattery. Was she mocking or commending him?

"I think I like you, Rowan of Deerskin," she spoke frankly, as if coming to a final conclusion. "I look forward to making this journey with you." She proceeded to pick up her step, pulling the map from her pack as she joined Farrow at the lead.

Rowan watched after her in bewilderment. She was pleased that he had defended someone that his tribe typically demeaned. This boded well for her addition to their group. Much as he did not want Jaela dragging him down, he did not desire the company of those who might make her way more difficult. A smirk nagged at the corner of his mouth as he watched the wind toss Elaine's long hair. He wasn't going to mind traveling with her either.

A sudden blow to his gut stole his breath away for some moments. Indignantly, he turned to his sister. *"What was that for?"*

Briar's expression was all innocence. "I was saving you from yourself, brother. If you are not careful, you might just fall for that golden head and then what will become of your ambitions?"

"I was just considering her as a traveling companion," he snapped.

"Yes?" she asked doubtfully. "And what do you make of her?"

"She... seems to approve of Jaela."

Briar glanced over her shoulder, causing Rowan to do the same. Jaela ambled some paces behind them. He wondered if it would be this way the whole of the journey—her lingering behind, holding them back. She peered up in surprise to find their eyes on her.

Briar waved to cover for their gawking, then turned to her brother. "Does Jaela require her approval?"

"What do you mean?"

"I do not see why we need Elaine's good opinion. She is not even supposed to be here."

"Well... it will make things easier, do not you think?"

She shrugged. *"Did* you mean all those things you said about Jaela at the assembly?"

"Why not?" Despite himself, he felt more confident concerning his decision knowing Elaine liked him for it.

"I never heard you defend her before. I just assumed you thought like the rest of us."

He turned his gaze on her. "Do you still think that way?"

Releasing a sigh, she shook her head. "I honestly never really thought about her before. She seems all right... but it *is* sort of unnerving that she breathes fire, you know?" When Rowan neglected to respond, she continued, "I never considered that her strangeness may have derived from the river people, like you suggested. It does put things in another light."

"It did not—" Rowan cut himself off, but it was too late.

Her eyes shot to his face. "Did not what? Is it not of Evange-line's blood? Why did you claim it was? And... how would *you* know, Ro?"

He shook his head. "It is a perplexing matter. Let us just take her for what she is and leave it at that, shall we?" He picked up his pace to walk beside Farrow. If he neglected to keep a close eye, they may be led along the wrong course. As it was, his own tongue seemed determined to lead him down unwanted paths.

⤜⤜⤜ ⤛⤛⤛

After a tedious day's trudging, Jaela stopped short as she entered the campsite Rowan and Elaine had selected. In the very midst of a large patch of briar bushes rested a small oasis consisting of a flat grassy patch of land. Beyond laughed a river fed by a waterfall in full view from their clearing. She had never seen water descend like this—had not even realized it could. There was a small section of rapid waters near their village, but that was the closest she had come to anything like this surging sheet of water that shimmered under the evening rays.

While the others positioned their belongings, Jaela remained stupefied by its magnificence. It was akin with her sentiments concerning Old Willow's roses. She wondered once again if this was what had moved the Great One to send her forth. Who was better acquainted with what could stir her soul?

The siblings took the initiative of building a fire while Farrow and Elaine discoursed quietly among themselves. Jaela couldn't help noticing that this bothered Briar. She was the true champion of Blooms. Elaine was only meant for a backup in case Briar did not follow through. But it was obvious that Farrow looked to Elaine as his cohort.

"Is there something I should be aware of?" Briar called across the clearing.

Elaine offered an easy smile, inviting her to sit beside them. "We were just exchanging stories of the danger that may be met along the way. It is not merely fractious tribes that are to be feared but... them."

"Them?" Briar pressed as she took a seat.

"Daemon sprites," Rowan informed as he arranged the tinder.

Briar looked to him with a start. "What danger could they pose out *here?* They should not be a concern until we reach the Nethers."

Farrow shook his head. "Grandmother Willow shared stories with Jethro and I..."

Jaela glanced up as if caught by sight of an arrow. Did he know what she had done to his grandmother? Nay, of course not. But she still felt uneasy at the mention of Old Willow... now a little less elderly.

"Farrow claims wicked sprites attack champions throughout the whole of the journey," Elaine explained with concern.

"But *why?*" Briar questioned. "They want us to deliver the recompense to their master, right?"

Farrow shook his head. "Grandmother says they would rather see the villages destroyed. Obstructing us from the finish, as you might say, is a favorite game. If they can stop us from completing the mission, they are free to wreak havoc."

"Then..." Elaine began thoughtfully, "why do we deliver it?"

Rowan was finally drawn to be seated with them. As his whole person reeked of concern, Jaela's anxiety increased as well. She searched the forestry. If daemonkind attempted to deter them from their mission within the forest, what happened when one entered their realm? It seemed an impossible feat. Yet, most of the clans had accomplished it for decades.

Farrow shrugged. "Grandmother claims it is wrong to deliver the recompense to the Nethers. She says we transgress by breaking ancient law ordained by the Creator, to whom the recompense was paid in prior days. She even tried to convince me to refuse the commissioning."

"If that is true..." Elaine began apprehensively, "when did it change?"

The group fell as silent as Jaela. It was all so convoluted. If the clans were delivering the recompense to the wrong place, why was it working? And why did daemonkind seek to stop them? Jaela's stomach turned in knots as she pondered this. The others proved to be thinking along the same lines as they broke the hush with further deliberations. But Jaela did not wish to hear any more. All she could stand to focus on was completing the quest, whatever it may mean, and returning home to Evangeline.

Meanwhile, the sky dimmed. Her fellow travelers would be famished when they broke from their discourse. She was hungry herself. Taking up a long twig, she instinctively blew it into flame. It wasn't long before the warmth of the bonfire permeated the cool evening. She was grateful for the small comfort, as well as the crackling that obscured much of what was discussed.

Perusing her supplies, she began preparation for their supper. Helping her mother fix morning and noon repasts had long been a favored pastime. It wasn't long before blistering, honey-glazed venison accompanied by roast vegetables sang delightful promise into the atmosphere. But it was the aroma of sweet dough baked on a number of spits that at last lured the group.

"Jaela of Deerskin," Elaine sounded as she surveyed the handiwork. "This is a *welcome* sight."

"I did not realize you could cook..." Briar spoke with mystification. "This looks fit for a tribe leader." She promptly seated herself beside Jaela, altogether skipping the venison for a first course of sticky, fluffy bread. "Mmhmmm," she sighed as if the cares of the world were rolled from her shoulders. "Rowan, you have to try this."

He sat down beside his sister, casting an appreciative nod to Jaela. "Seems we left you with all the work. Thanks for this." He helped himself to a steaming piece of fall-apart venison. His eyes closed the moment it met his tongue.

"Here, *here,*" Farrow interjected of a sudden.

Of the group, he was the most difficult to induce a reaction from. His approval inspired her wonderment. She had never considered that cooking well might earn her a true place among them.

Once the majority was consumed, Jaela was the first to prepare her bedroll. It had been a long day. Her muscles protested against the unaccustomed treatment but were summarily soothed as she lay down. The others followed suit, though intermittent discourse soon followed.

"Rowan says he will not marry until he has made a name for himself," Briar divulged as they discussed future hopes. "Though there is a girl at home who claims him."

Jaela wondered if Briar had noticed her brother's attentiveness to Elaine. Was her comment a cantankerous poke? Jaela smirked at the thought.

Rowan proceeded to snort. "Caspa is of no interest to me."

"Well, I have similar notions," Elaine confided. "It is why I was so eager for the chance to come along. Any opportunity for adventure. I want to *see* things."

"Jethro would not like to hear that," Farrow put in with a dry laugh. "He has been nutty about you for ages."

Elaine chuckled. "Your brother is nutty about every girl."

Jaela chortled inwardly. So, her first interested party was an easy catch. That explained it. Yet... he *had* favored her over the dauntless Briar. That was something. As she gazed past the moonlit treetops and into the lustrous galaxy overhead, she wondered if anyone would ever favor her in such a way again.

Hearing their shared remarks, she wished she might murmur a "celestial twilight," to feel herself a part of them and not apart from them. But despite their approval of the meal, it was precisely how it must always be due to her impediment.

She could not help asking herself once more what her purpose was here. Where was her Great Friend in all this? Could she accomplish what he desired... especially when she had no idea what that was? She was not even altogether certain he was watching. But she had trusted him this far. She would do so for as long as faith permitted.

It was difficult to tell the time of night when Jaela awoke with a start. Her eyes widened as she watched the bluish flame emit softly from her mouth. She had been speaking in her sleep. Had this ever occurred before? She feared the others had seen. But as she listened in stillness, it was clear they slept on. So, why was she awake?

It seemed an age she lay with her blood heated as if from an impulse. To her utter relief, nothing arose from it. She turned one way and then another and still she was wakeful. With a sigh, she gazed into the outer atmosphere. The moon shone brightly. She feared it would soon be morning and she would have gained no further rest.

She sat upright as something darkened her view, sending a cold chill through her body. In the next moment, all was clear. She nearly laid back down when a moan from Briar demanded her attention.

By the softest illumination of dying embers, a pair of lurking shadows were revealed. Briar whimpered like a small child in the clutches of some foe. Was it a silhouette or mere shadow? Jaela strained her eyes to make out the dark mass.

She was frozen with chills as they raced up and down her body. It was all she could do not to shriek over the humanoid creature that clutched Briar, its talon-like hands pierced into her scalp. The sleeping girl released another cry. A gasp from Farrow revealed he was in the grips of a like being.

"What do you think are you doing?" Jaela hissed into the darkness. The words were out before she realized what she was about.

Two gleaming pairs of eyes darted to her in astonishment. Releasing their victims, they started toward her. She scrambled back until the briar bushes caught her in their own claws. Though the discomfort provoked a yelp of pain, she embraced them as the creatures loomed.

"What *are* you?" she squealed in terror.

The nearest one fell back with a hiss as her fire wafted into its face. Jaela was stunned by this development. Her flame did not typically burn flesh. The only thing she had ever so much as singed was wood. She blinked back at the second creature as it considered her. Though it appeared intent upon flight, she felt her blood smolder.

"No," she whispered against the impulse.

She bounded to her feet, brazenly advancing behind the flaming bursts that accompanied her imperceptible language. She could in no way fathom what was articulated, nor why her seemingly inept tongue produced such effect on these adversaries. The ghoulish persons became ablaze with blue and green flame, screeching and writhing in torment. Large black wings materialized from their backs to carry them off like a pair of oversized bats.

After a moment, Jaela's blood cooled and her tongue fell silent. The horror of the incident sent her scrambling for the comfort of her bedroll. She tossed fresh kindling into the bonfire before tugging the coverlet tightly about her form. Once the fire was ablaze, she searched the treetops for further danger. *Anything* might be lurking. But what had those things been?

Elder Si's counsels returned like a blow to her gut. *Daemonkind.* Though the group was yet so far from their lair, the group had already encountered them. But what had been their purpose with the defenseless sleepers? Had they harmed them? She abandoned her bedroll to survey Briar. Her breathing was even and restful. Her face appeared valiant even in sleep. Farrow, too, breathed evenly. They were well.

She returned to her bed. It was clear this was no journey to be simply endured so one could move on. It was to be survived tooth and nail. To her estimation, they were at war with the very realm to which they were destined. No wonder there were those who never returned. Yet...

Lifting a hand before her face, she breathed into it. Her fire was warm but did not burn. It felt rather invigorating. In the past, it had healed. With Old Willow, it reversed her years. Tonight, however, it had proved a weapon against these dark forces. *She,* insignificant Jaela of Deerskin, had sent them to flight.

CHAPTER 12

As THE RAYS OF the morning kissed Rowan's skin, he rolled himself from his bed to survey the encampment. All were accounted for. That was fortunate. He had intended to suggest they organize shifts to keep watch in the night. Jaela appeared to have had the same notion as she sat with knees tucked close to her chest, gazing into the dead fire.

"Celestial sunrise?" he questioned.

Her weary eyes widened for some moments as if disputing the matter. In the end, she nodded.

Proceeding to refold his bedroll, he kicked himself for having left such a responsibility to the last person he would have expected to be mindful of it. Perhaps she would prove no deadweight after all.

"Oh, I had the *vilest* dream last night," Briar grumbled as she sat up. "I was *ill* and *feverish*." She rubbed at her arms as if she were cold. "It felt so real that I half believed I was sick before I opened my eyes just now."

"Thank the Creator, you are not," Rowan replied evenly.

She nodded in meditation. "There was this toasty light in the end. It enveloped me like... like the rays of the sun. It soothed my aches and fever..."

"I dreamed as well," Farrow put in as he set to work on the morning meal. "I was afraid. Mm... more like petrified." He shook his head. "I have never felt anything like it before."

"What did you fear?" Elaine questioned as she aided his efforts with their repast.

He brooded some moments before, "The passage into the Nethers. I was determined to race home to Blooms. I felt something like an echo of it as I awoke." He shivered unconsciously.

"Well, I am glad you are still here," Elaine answered with a small smile. "The tribe would be lost without you."

"*Thanks,*" Briar muttered over her cold tea.

"But as with Briar..." Farrow continued, "there was a light—all flickery and shimmering."

Briar nodded as she set down her beverage. "Strange."

Rowan pondered this happenstance. It was unusual they should both endure nightmares allayed by the same light. The clans believed dreams possessed messages. If it was so with these, what did they portend?

His attention was diverted by Jaela's abrupt exit from the clearing. With an inward sigh, he drew to his feet and started after her. He did not plan on letting her out of his sight again. Creeping silently within the shadows, he wondered what she could be about. He supposed she would have informed them if she were able. She would appear less mysterious that way. In the end, she was merely refilling her waterskin. To his surprise, she filled his and Briar's as well.

He was distracted by her thoughtfulness when she stood and turned about. Astonishment at finding him there provoked a shriek from her lips, accompanied by flame that emerged as a shooting star in lavender glow. He had never observed her fire so close before. If it was not such a disconcerting manifestation, it would be resplendent. He nearly made mention of it before catching sight of the blood on her arms.

"What is *this?*" he questioned, grasping one of them.

She peered back into his face with wide eyes.

"Has someone harmed you? Was it Farrow?" Though the fellow seemed quiet and collected, Rowan harbored fears he might be like some of the other young clansfolk, who would not bat an eye at taunting someone like Jaela.

She shook her head, eyeing his tight grasp on her arm.

With an apology, he released it. She motioned for him to follow her. When they returned to the campsite, she pointed to the briar bushes. His brows rose with understanding.

"I see..." he answered. "Well, be sure to pat some salve on those wounds. They look deep." He proceeded to pull a thorn from her flesh. "On second thought, have a seat."

If she could not even care for herself in the small things, how was he to keep her safe when they met real danger? Taking his brimming waterskin in hand, he used it to wash the blood away, removing a number of briars in the process.

"You cannot simply leave things like this to fester," he informed irritably as he applied the salve. "I understand you are not much interested in your appearance, but this is something that could cause further trouble in future."

Glancing up in time to catch her pained expression, he noticed she had taken the time to comb her hair again. It managed to make her comelier. He almost regretted the comment but could not help feeling it important that she represent their tribe well.

Drawing to his feet, he noticed Elaine and Farrow had nearly completed the morning meal. From the looks of it, they were in for charred fish. Thankfully, he had eaten more than his fair share the evening prior. The group proceeded to consume their bounty in silence, none wishing to speak the obvious.

Elaine took the initiative. "We are not the best cooks…"

Farrow shrugged as he continued to eat hardily. "It is food." Venturing a glance in Jaela's direction, he added, "Last night's was a masterpiece."

Jaela blushed as she consumed her burned portions. Rowan grumbled inwardly. He had feared Farrow's harm. Now, he dreaded the annoyance of a budding romance. It was one thing when Jethro showed her attention back in the village. But this was a grave quest. They must all be on their toes. Still, Jaela could not speak. That would certainly slow things should they be heading in that direction. As for himself, he refused to admit he had entertained interest concerning Elaine only the day prior. She was stunning and stouthearted, to be sure. But his focus was better spent on the mission.

Jaela spent the remainder of the day much like the previous. She followed the others, studying and learning them as best she could from her vantage apart from them. It was clear Farrow was uncomfortable with Briar as a fellow champion. He spoke to her as little as possible, preferring Elaine's company. And who could blame him? Elaine was so amiable that even Rowan found her difficult to resist.

Though Rowan sought Farrow's companionship, the somber fellow proved mostly uncommunicative. This left only Briar and Elaine for company. Jaela easily perceived that he worked to keep his focus on his sister, but Elaine was difficult to ignore. Jaela pondered the possibility of a relationship between the two and decided she much preferred it to the notion of him with Caspa.

It was surprising how well Briar and Elaine got on. It could only be because they shared similar dogmas that Briar was able to overcome the affrontery of the back-up champion's presence. Jaela craved to enter their company, but what could she do but watch and listen? That was managed much less ambiguously at the rear of the party.

Her mind often drifted to the events of the evening before. Each time the faces of those vile sprites entered her mind, she trembled with horror at ever encountering them again. It mattered not that she had prevailed. It had not really been her doing. And the position her impulsive tongue had placed her in was frightening. It was enough that she lost control of her own body from time to time, but it had occurred regularly the last few days. Now, she had been compelled to assail the phantoms of nightmares.

The slowly changing terrain gradually liberated her from such meditations. It was stimulating to come upon trees she had never seen before. Large, rounded trunks that appeared ages old towered far overheard. Here and there were scattered patches of galeria, a flowering weed with long-tendrilled petals that drifted when the wind blew but drooped miserably without it. Mossy rock-formations materialized haphazardly as well. As Farrow bounded from rock to rock, Jaela longed to join him but did not relish drawing attention to herself.

It was the sparkling pool swallowed by the mouth of an enormous grotto that stopped the company in their tracks. Bright green vegetation draped long, lacy fingers over the uppermost crest from which water filtered blithely into the water below. To Jaela, it appeared like something out of a dream.

With a contented sigh, Farrow removed his pack and dropped upon the shore. "I do not know about you all, but this is my campground for the evening."

Elaine shook her head. "The map says we are expected to take shelter within the nearest village. It is not far now."

Farrow waved a careless hand at her. "Is this paradise not good enough for the likes of the beloved Elaine of Blooms?"

"I am with Farrow," Rowan interjected. "Too much time is wasted within the villages. I have a mind to skip them altogether." When he carefully avoided Jaela's gaze, she wondered if it was due to her that he wished to avoid encountering more people.

"But I am eager to meet other tribes," Elaine pressed.

"This is not a jaunt, Elaine," Farrow chastised. "Haste is key."

"I have never understood why champions are not released with more time to spare," Briar put in as she dropped her pack beside Farrow's.

"The portal to the Nethers is only open for a short time," Rowan explained. "And the more time spent away from home, the greater opportunity for endangerment."

"Portal?" Briar questioned. "What is that?"

It was clear that Rowan had not intended on revealing he knew more about this journey than most. "I cannot claim to truly understand it.... There seems to be a kind of light that instantly transports one from our realm to the Nethers."

"You mean the Nethers is not a..." Elaine searched for the right words as she sat down beside Briar, clearly given to her fate beside the grotto. "A land upon Kaern?"

Rowan shrugged. "That is how my great grandfather described it."

Briar nodded. "I never knew Grandfather, but I have heard tales that the Nethers is found deep within the core of our world. Perhaps it is not a plane we could enter by mere walking."

As the four exchanged myths, Jaela resolved to prepare the evening meal. Briar and Elaine had concocted an almost inedible dish at noontime, to say nothing of the charred fish for breakfast. None seemed eager to try again. Ergo, she planned a fortifying soup. Her eyes sparkled when she spotted a patch of rig's herb nearby. This was a favorite seasoning that was difficult to come by back home.

"How can I help?" Rowan asked as he knelt beside her in the brush.

She leaped with surprise. Must he always approach without warning?

"I apologize," he mumbled with mild amusement, proceeding to help her gather the herb.

She was pleased with how much they collected. Though she wished to pluck every bit of it for their future meals, she settled for half.

At the fireside, Rowan spoke quietly, "I am not a bad cook—huntsman's honor." He put a hand to his chest.

She averted her eyes, unable to picture him ever having stepped into a kitchen. Moreover, she did not know how to guide him through her process.

He persisted as if it were a secret, "I have aided my mother a number of times. By the way the cooking has been going, you will be on your own with every meal if you do not accept my aid."

Her eyes lit on his face. Rowan, of all people, truly wished to help her with the cooking. Why did it not suit her suppositions of him? Blinking away confusion, she took up the only pot in their larder and started for the pool. Abruptly, she turned back and ventured to point out her mound of vegetables.

"A soup?" he questioned as he reached for his dagger.

She nodded.

It was nice having someone willing to help. She would not in the least mind if she was expected to prepare every meal for the remainder. It gave her something to amuse herself while allowing her to pull her weight on an expedition for which she was ill-fitted. But company was something she craved. She would not turn her nose up at it.

Rowan had already completed his task upon her return. At her direction, he moved on to the smoked rabbits, taking the time to shred them into neat chunks. Jaela acknowledged that he worked as if from experience. Apparently, he was adept at everything. She might have sighed in frustration if she were not a little proud to be in his company.

In a short time, there were "oohs" and "aahs" from the others as they appreciated the smoky, viscous broth with tender meat and hardy vegetables.

"I meant to mention this last evening," Rowan began near the end of the supper. "It would be shrewd to keep night watches. Say, two watchman per night on rotation through the evenings to come?"

Elaine nodded. "I should have thought of that. We are a fortunate group to have so many to keep shifts."

"Jaela volunteered hers last night," Rowan informed, "so she is off for tonight."

Jaela blinked at the recognition given her. She had not intended to post guard. It had been the discovery that there were enemies in the camp that had put her on edge. How could one sleep when they knew what was out there? How would she sleep this evening, watchman or not?

"I will take first shift," Briar volunteered. "I am not weary in the least."

"I claim second," Farrow informed.

Before long, Jaela lay in the silence of the night. As the evening was warmer, the fire had been put out. Yet, the moon softly illuminated the world, producing murky shadows. What if they should have visitors again? Would Briar be able to handle them? With a snort, she turned over. This was *Briar* she was considering.

She had not realized she'd relented to slumber until she was jolted to consciousness. With a startled gasp, she discovered Briar shaking her. Jaela scrambled to sit up, eyes darting about for danger.

"You were talking in your sleep," Briar informed. "I... did not know if you might inadvertently light the forest on fire or something."

Jaela grumbled inwardly. Did she often do this without knowing or was it somehow triggered by this mission? Her mother had never said anything. Either way, it was humiliating. She shook her head to intimate it would not be a problem.

"All right..." Briar answered softly. "Sorry."

Jaela lay back again. It was some time before she could relax enough to nod off, but the flapping of wings sent her bolt upright. To her horror, there proved an even larger daemon sprite than those of the last evening. It towered behind Briar where she rested against a tree. Before Jaela could think what to do, the creature planted talons into their watchman's head. Briar did not seem to be aware of the occurrence. Instead, her head bobbed to confirm she had nodded off.

Jaela wasted no time in scrambling to her feet and surrendering the words she could not translate even of herself. She knew she was not in control. This was an impulse. But this time she was grateful. The sprite released its grip.

It vaulted for Jaela, fury smoldering in its humanoid eyes. As Jaela flew back, it hooked her foot with a sharp talon that sent grief up her leg. She heard her language spill out like a stream that engulfed the vile creature. It was soon squealing upon the ground much as she had just done.

Her tongue did not desist. The daemon was granted no opportunity to flee like her previous foes. She began to question what would happen if her comrades awoke to find a deceased daemon in the middle of their site. Of a sudden, the creature burst into a mound of ash.

Jaela stood breathing over the enigma. She had not realized she could do *this*. But how should she handle the remains? Leave them for the others to question? Yes, that was best. It was her only means of warning them that things were not right.

As if reading her mind, a mighty gust swirled through the expanse, playing at her hair and clothes as it passed. With purpose, it swept up the ashes, carrying them off into the night. Jaela folded her arms as she returned to her bedroll.

What could that have been about? It was her one chance of notifying the others. Or was she expected to remain vigilant every night? She might have written it off as a chance of nature if the sensation of the wind had not felt something like HS. But if he was truly about, why was he ignoring her? He had promised to be with her, to care for her, and here she had been forced to defend the camp two nights in a row. He wasn't angry with her, surely. For his sake, she had agreed to something that terrified her, but he had not spoken a word since.

Even so... as she considered the last few days, she realized they had been as pleasant as could be expected. Things she would have previously dreaded were proving curiously bearable. Perhaps that was his doing. Yet, these daemons lurked and if he had appeared at all, it was merely to sweep away her mess.

Once again, she had to ask herself what precisely these creatures intended. Why had this one put Briar to sleep while she was meant to be on watch? Was it a personal target against Briar or had it meant to send further danger with no guard on hand? She shivered at the thought. Thus far, they seemed only intent on affecting them with nightmares. But she had no idea how far these creatures could or would go... What might happen if she did not awaken to their presence some time in future? What would happen if she *did?*

CHAPTER 13

ROWAN SHOOK HIS HEAD as he prepared the morning meal alongside Jaela. She had not slept. In fact, Briar admitted to falling asleep during her shift. No one had even awoken Farrow for his.

"Thank you for keeping watch again," he grumbled in a low voice.

Jaela nodded as if she scarcely heard him.

"But you should have wakened Farrow."

She flashed dark eyes at him before returning them to her work.

"Can you not sleep?" he ventured.

"I woke her up," Briar admitted with remorse.

He turned to her with irritation. *"Why?"*

Briar and Jaela locked eyes a moment. The latter appeared like a deer in sight of an arrow.

"She... was dreaming," Briar claimed.

"Dreams cannot harm one," Rowan censured. "Let her sleep next time."

His sister merely nodded while Jaela's hands worked all the more fiercely. It seemed to him there was more to this story, but he would let it slide. If Briar felt something should remain unspoken, he trusted that.

For the remainder of the day, Jaela struggled to keep up. Rowan fell back to keep stride with her. There was no other choice. They could not run the risk of falling behind schedule. The two would make a laughing stock if he opted to carry her, much as he was tempted. Two nights without sleep wasn't going to cut it. He would be hanged if there was a third.

"I will take the watch tonight," he assured her.

She did not appear comforted. Instead, her eyes widened with fright.

"What is it?" he pressed, realizing something was wrong. "Do you fear the nightmares?"

She shook her head.

He ran a hand through his hair. If only he had long ago admitted in all honesty that he could understand her speech. She grasped his arm to draw his attention and proceeded with a series of gestures.

He shook his head to indicate he grasped nothing. "Try again," he encouraged.

She did so to no avail.

Before long, Elaine drew beside them. "Something wrong?"

Jaela ceased her attempts with a sigh.

"Seems to be," Rowan answered with apprehension. "But I cannot begin to make it out."

"Can I try?" she inquired of Jaela.

Jaela appeared both self-conscious and frustrated but eventually began again.

"Something... with wings?" Elaine tried.

Jaela nodded as if she could hug her.

"Some animal?" Rowan tried.

She shook her head, persisting with gestures that not even Elaine could work out.

"It was likely some new kind of animal," Rowan assured in the end. "Something specific to the region. It seems we remain untouched as yet. That is promising."

Jaela shook her head but refused to continue with the dissatisfying game.

"Well... we cannot have you lagging like this," Rowan began in a tone he hoped would settle the matter. "I will take a longer shift to make certain you get your rest."

Her plain dissatisfaction did nothing for his ego.

Though Rowan did not expect trouble, he stood resolute upon his feet that night. Briar had admitted to nodding off on the job. He was of no mind to follow suit.

It was convenient to boast the protection that a larger company provided, but the responsibility of protecting so many weighed heavily on him. As no one had implied it was his burden to carry, he had no notion from where it came. Short of Briar, he had not experienced it before. And though he had hoped such sentiment would be restricted to those from his own tribe, Elaine and Farrow were growing on him. They were his sort—namely Elaine.

In his mind, she was everything a young woman should be. She wielded weapons, hunted, fished and shared ambitions along the lines of his own. She was *him*... as a female. But she was also considerate toward someone like Jaela. That kind of thoughtfulness was a rare quality among the tribes. Though he had been raised to think it a weakness, it seemed to place her somewhere above the rest of the clanspeople. He was surprised to find himself drawn to it.

But he could not entertain such notions—not if he was to achieve all he had dreamed since he was a boy. Maybe one day, when he had garnered the kind of position he sought, he might be fortunate enough to find her available to pursue. For now, he was grateful that, though she often sought his company and seemed to like him, she remained aloof. This was completely different from anything he had learned to expect. He was accustomed to females falling at his feet.

Of course, Jaela had never done so either, but she was different... as was *Elaine*. And he liked the Blooms girl all the more for it. He could know her as a comrade before being turned off by the adoration he was so accustomed to.

A chill ran down his back as something brushed his arm. Twirling about, he caught sight of a passing shadow. Swiftly, he notched an arrow. He listened in stillness. Nothing. With a sigh of relief, he nearly restored the arrow when a form stepped into the camp.

"Hey!" he thundered, releasing his arrow into the side a foul creature that clutched Jaela in its freakishly humanoid arms. To his astonishment, the projectile passed through its body, landing close beside Jaela. With a head bobbed as if with confusion, the creature's gaze shot to him. Slowly, its frown became a snarling grin as another of its kind landed in the middle of the camp. This one lost no time in taking Briar into its clutches.

Rowan notched another arrow, releasing it. He did so again to no avail. Briar whimpered but remained slumbering. What *were* these things and what harm did they pose? How was he supposed to defend his camp against flesh that his arrows refused to catch?

With no other option, he launched toward the one clutching his sister and consequently fell through it. Briar cried out, writhing in the creature's arms, though she remained unconscious.

Seeing he could not physically reach these monsters, Rowan decided upon another tactic. He flung himself over his sister's form, placing his own hands where the creature's were. He succeeded in instigating its fury but was summarily batted away like a child's doll. Leaping to his feet, Rowan roared a challenge, hoping to alert the others to the danger. The beast did not seem eager to have him awaken the company. It shrieked into the atmosphere before thrusting him against a nearby tree.

Rowan's stomach dropped as the sound of many wings preempted the throng of dark beasts that landed in the encampment. With difficulty, he drew to his feet again.

Suddenly, the voice of the one holding Jaela called out, "You there, seize the last two. *You,* help me keep the firetongue under. She's the only threat. The rest of you, after *him."* It pointed directly at Rowan. "He's more trouble than we bargained for. Mind, he can see you. I don't know how! The girl was supposed to be the only one."

Rowan's eyes bulged as five of them bolted for him. He heard himself cry out in response to the attack of their clawed fists and feet. He possessed enough coherency to question how they affected his physical form when he could not reach theirs. Before long, he couldn't have cared less. If only he might escape these brutalities such as he had never endured in his life. If only he might live to tell about it.

A blistering roar wrenched Jaela from her slumber. It was not until she felt the soreness of her throat that she realized it had sounded from herself. Her eyes flew open upon feeling herself restrained to her bedroll. A set of daemons returned her gaze with widening eyes.

"She wasn't supposed to awaken!" the first bellowed. "I said *keep her under!"*

An impulse was at work, boiling fiercely within Jaela's blood, filling her with unaccustomed rage. The creature slapped its disgusting hand over her mouth. She tasted putrid membrane that she attempted to chomp to no avail. She felt herself slipping under again.

Suddenly, she caught what she had perceived in her sleep—whimpering. *Rowan*. She wrenched her head to the side to witness the abuses he suffered before her captor yanked her back. They would kill him if someone did not do something.

Her eyes became slits as they fixed on the daemon. For the first time in her life, she welcomed her brooding impulse, allowing its intentions to become hers. She sensed a rumbling in her throat. Her tongue clicked within the entrapment of her mouth. She felt the pressure build. By the time the daemon's eyes bulged in realization of what occurred, it was too late.

"Shut her down, you half-wit!" it screamed before her mouth exploded with blazing inferno, thoroughly roasting her captors.

The next moment, she was marching toward Rowan's abusers. *"In the name of I Am, the Creator of all things, including your sorry hides..."* she bellowed in her mind, though what emerged might have been anything. She knew the words were not her own. In fact, she scarcely understood what was transpiring. *"I command you to depart from our company this instant!"*

The band froze and looked to her as if uncertain of what to do. Their glances fell to her bedroll in search of the ones who had held her. Finding none, they faltered. Finally, first one and then another started for her.

"I said *nooow!"* she rumbled.

Torrential flames engulfed those nearest. The rest were frozen in place beside Rowan, loath to leave their task unfinished. Two still clutched him as if they would carry him off.

Before Jaela knew it, a fresh impulse brewed, releasing a deluge of words that she in no way processed. The language was accompanied by flaming arrows that pierced her enemies like shooting stars. Upon hitting their mark, each creature exploded into ash. Those who remained took to rapid flight.

As she sensed her impulsive behavior waning, she took the liberty of calling out, "And do not dare return to us again, *you slivering snakes!*"

It was good to feel powerful.

Of a sudden, she recalled the sprites who had clutched the remainder of their group. She spun to find them vanished as well. Moreover, her comrades were wide awake.

"What goes on here?" Farrow fairly bellowed.

"Where is Rowan?" Briar questioned, eyes darting about.

A moan sounded from where Rowan lay. Jaela raced to his side, Briar at her tail.

"*Rowan!*" the sister shrieked, falling beside him to pat at his swelling wounds as if wishing to help without knowing how. "What have you *done* to him?" she thundered into Jaela's face. Without warning, Briar tackled her to the ground, prepared to strike.

"*Stop,*" Rowan croaked. "Was not... her. She *saved...*"

They returned to his side as his words sputtered into a choke that filled Jaela with trepidation. Unconsciously, she pushed the bloody, matted hair from his forehead. His eyes found hers.

"If I do not make it..."

"Do not *say* it!" Briar shrieked.

He shook his head, eyes still on Jaela. "Watch out... for..." His gaze went to Briar.

Jaela wished she could implore him to hold on. This wasn't how things were supposed to go. He was the strong one, the capable one. *She* was the one who was not supposed to return.

Elaine and Farrow knelt at Rowan's feet.

"He is *not...?*" Elaine began, eyes pooling with tears.

Jaela's brows furrowed as she turned from them to gaze back at Rowan. He still looked to her, as if awaiting a response. Her blood sparked. She welcomed it, urging the fresh impulse to help him, hoping beyond hope that was the intention.

CHAPTER 14

ROWAN WAS ENGULFED IN welcome heat from Jaela's flaring utterances. Briar rose as if to stop her, but he clutched his sister's arm with what little strength remained. She could not know what Jaela spoke. Perhaps even Jaela was unaware. She certainly did not appear like herself. She was like an angel of legend with hair made luminous by her flame. Her eyes smoldered like shimmering honey. Power and serenity resided there. He clung to it like a mother's embrace.

"By the power of the Great One, the Creator of all things," he perceived from her mouth, "I command healing into your form, Rowan of Deerskin, Rowan the Defender, Rowan of the forthcoming Great Archipelagos. I summon angels of healing into this expanse to cleanse you of all daemonic abuses and of every lie, scar and incantation."

A flock of shooting stars appeared in the heavens overhead, plummeting toward them like a broken, blazing meteorite. In a breath, the humanoid beings with wings landed in the expanse.

Rowan questioned if he was dreaming as they generated the sweetest music he had ever known.

Though they possessed mysterious similarities to the dark creatures, these were everything the others had not been. They shone as with the glory of a thousand Celestial Spectacles. He watched in mystification as they danced around him. The warmth in his body intensified and it was not unpleasant.

His eyes re-fixed upon Jaela's shining ones as she spoke as if in a trance, "Rowan of Deerskin, there approaches a day when the one who is Faithful and True will make himself vulnerable to cruelties such as you have endured this night. He intends to take every scar, malady and wrongdoing upon himself and carry it into death."

Rowan could not begin to comprehend what this meant, what it had to do with him, why he should care. His mind scrambled for understanding.

"Rowan... he will save you," she continued.

His heart pounded with the avowal.

"You will be cleansed, you will be whole, you will be free... so pledges the Great One."

Suddenly, his eyes drooped. He felt his muscles soothe and settle. Was he merely giving way to rest or relinquishing his spirit to the afterlife? He could not say. His eyes shot to Briar in order to utter a final farewell, but the words died on his lips.

⤞⤞⤞ ⬳⬳⬳

Jaela's tongue rested as she felt the impulse depart. Rowan's head nodded to the side with a final breath. Her heart pounded. His chest rose in the next moment and then fell with an evenness that denoted slumber. She scanned his face, his head, arms, legs. He appeared *well*. He had been on the brink of death and now, from what she could tell, his wounds were mended. Had her strange speech truly done all this?

But what had she *said?* She never knew what was emitted from her lips—only what her mind intended. But in singular situations such as this, personal intentions had no space. Something else had possession of her. She began to question just what or who was the culprit.

Could it... could it be that *HS,* the spirit-essence of the Great One himself, dwelled within her somehow? It was unfeasible. Yet, it *would* mean she was never alone; he had promised that. But... this would make her something like a home to him, a sanctuary of sorts. She shook her head at the impossibility.

"Oh, *Jaela...*" Briar whispered hoarsely. "Look what you did... You *healed* him." She stroked his arm that, moments before, had been bloody and bruised.

"All right..." Farrow drew to his feet to glare at Jaela. "Who *are* you?"

"They said she was the offspring of Evangeline," Elaine reminded. "She possesses the blood of the river people."

"Sure," he began doubtfully, "but have you ever heard tales of a river person having done anything like *that.*" He gestured to Rowan's mended frame. "It is not natural."

"No, it is *not,*" Briar interjected. "It is extraordinary." She looked to Jaela. "I am so sorry I never—never understood you. I should have tried to know you... But *thank you* for mending Rowan."

"How can we be certain she did not harm him in the first place?" Farrow persisted, eyeing Jaela with suspicion. *"What happened?"*

"We were attacked..." Jaela let the words die on her tongue as he flew back in fear of her flame. How was she to explain?

"That is quite enough, Farrow," Elaine snapped. "Let us leave them be. We will return to our beds and gain what rest we may yet. It is clear some of us need it." She nodded to Jaela and Briar as she urged Farrow on. Her questioning eyes lingered just a moment longer on Jaela.

Briar released a sigh. "You should sleep too, Jaela. I will stay with him."

Jaela shook her head. What if the daemons returned despite her order? She was only Jaela of Deerskin after all.

"You know he would want you to." Briar gestured to Rowan. "He will worry if you appear weary when next he sees you."

Jaela scanned his peacefully slumbering form. He slept like a newborn infant. It was the most pleasant she had ever seen him look, making her reluctant to leave. She ran her fingers through his hair, stopping short as she realized what she did. She refused to meet Briar's eye in pursuit of whether she thought the action appropriate. She and Rowan were scarcely acquaintances, let alone friends. Yet, she felt a tie pulling on her as she retreated from his side. Her heart turned fiercely as she recalled the sound of his cries. She turned over in her bedroll in an effort to drown them out.

She reminded herself that he had gone from a daemonic thrashing to serene slumber in a matter of moments. He would be well... thanks to the gift the Great One had bestowed upon her. For the first time in her life, she was obliged. The notion that Rowan would have died without it sent a turn to her chest like nothing she had ever felt before.

The firetongue lay awake for what felt like hours, reliving the episode moment by moment. Though she should be exhausted, she felt peculiarly energized. Excitement filled her lungs each time she took a breath. She had protected her camp, saved herself, healed Rowan. All this was accomplished with the gift she had loathed the whole of its existence—the one she had consciously and unconsciously blamed HS for giving her. As much as she had loved him, and attempted to trust his judgement, she now realized she had suffered a wound concerning his actions in her life. The gift had made her the scorned of her community. She had felt herself all wrong, wanting and a waste of resources upon Deerskin.

Now, she felt *formidable*... at least to daemonkind. And could this... could it be her purpose— her purpose on this journey and in her life in general? Had *she*—defenseless, fragile, useless Jaela—been made to be a daemon-slayer? She almost chuckled at the ludicrous concept. But... for the first time in her life, she made sense.

She awoke to a blaring noon-day sun. Her muscles ached but her spirit was strangely at peace. The events of the evening gradually unfolded in her memory. She had saved Rowan of Deerskin. She had a purpose. She wasn't altogether certain what that was, but she no longer believed herself cursed. She was gifted. Her unique language performed miracles.

"About time, sleepy angel," Briar greeted as Jaela sat up with a yawn. "Hungry?" She passed her a piece of smoked venison. "We opted not to cook anything... Seemed like a waste of supplies to try."

Jaela accepted the meat, nibbling on it as she rose to her feet. Where was Rowan?

Briar gestured to where he yet lay, not an inch from where he had drifted off the night before. "He has not awoken as yet. I would be concerned if you had not slept late, as well."

Jaela tried to resist anxiety, but the persistent serenity of his rest appeared strange to her. His breathing was too deep, too even—precisely as it had been before. She shook off these questions. She must trust the one who spoke through her.

Forcing her eyes from Rowan, she turned in search of Farrow and Elaine.

Briar shrugged. "Hunting. They do not like to sit still."

Jaela nodded as she sat down to finish her venison.

"Hard to believe we all thought you were cursed," Briar spoke quietly after some moments. She met Jaela's eye. "I mean... I *really* thought you were a freak—a 'wild thing,' like everyone said." She shook her head, casting her gaze to the glowing green of the forest. "You are much like Rowan claimed—someone akin to an angel."

Jaela shook her head, uncomfortable with the comparison.

"No, *truly*. I mean, I understand you are not *really* an angel. But... your mother always said you spoke in their tongue. Maybe... maybe she is right."

Jaela did not openly disagree, but she felt certain her speech was like no idiom known to any but HS. In fact, he had once told her as much—that only he and one other could translate her words. She had questioned to whom he referred, but he had refused to indulge her.

"At any rate..." Briar continued, "thank you again. I cannot tell you how dear my brother is to me. I was in no way prepared to lose him. My parents would thank you, as well, if they knew."

It was remarkable to receive such thanks and commendation from Briar, of all people. Jaela had looked up to her for so long, longed to be something like her. Indeed, she had ached to have her, have *anyone,* for a friend. Now, Briar looked upon her with a kind of awe. Jaela proceeded to squeeze the girl's hand where it lay on her ankle. It was the only means she had of responding. She was not even certain what it was meant to convey. Perhaps... a thanks for now seeing her as someone other than what the tribe had deemed her.

The two spent the afternoon in obscured converse. Briar spoke while Jaela responded with facial expressions. Briar did not seem to mind. It was clear she liked to chatter.

Elaine and Farrow popped in now and then to ask after Rowan's progress. When each time they discovered that he yet slumbered, it was clear some unspoken argument was taking place between them. At evening meal, only Briar and Elaine conversed. Farrow consumed the bounty Jaela had prepared readily enough, but he often cast glances at Rowan and then Jaela.

Finally, Elaine voiced the question that none would speak. "When do you expect him to awaken?"

Briar shrugged. "I wager he will be right as rain come morning. He was on the brink of death, if you recall."

Elaine nodded. "But... I thought you healed him?" Her gaze went to Jaela.

Jaela contemplated this for the hundredth time. It was true that he appeared well, but his eerily tranquil sleep made her uneasy. Wouldn't a healed person wake up? But he breathed on. That was something. In the end, she shrugged. How could she ever hope to explain something she did not grasp herself?

By noon the following day, Farrow spoke up. "I understand he is not dead... but eternal sleep is not going to do him any good either."

"He will not sleep *forever*," Briar scolded, crossing her arms. "If he has not awoken, he must require the rest."

"But we must be moving on," Farrow asserted in a low voice.

Briar blinked back. "Seriously? You do not possess patience enough to let his strength return?"

"I thought he was healed," he defended. "Can we not wake him up?"

Briar's mouth opened before faltering. She stood to examine Rowan's frame, which had not moved a single muscle from where he had initially nodded off. "Should we?" she asked of Jaela.

Jaela began to shake her head before shrugging. She could not ascertain why he slept on. Perhaps it would be better to awaken him.

Briar knelt beside her brother. "Rowan," she murmured.

Nothing.

Once more, she called with boldness.

Not the twitching of an eyelid.

"*Ro?*" she shouted with a shake to his arm.

No response.

Her eyes flew to Jaela.

Jaela crept beside him in order to shake him more forcefully. "Wake up," she urged.

His eyelids spasmed. She nearly opened her mouth to speak again when Briar took to patting his cheeks and shouting his name into the treetops. Jaela licked her lips. Would her speech, her fire, reach him?

"*Do not,*" she perceived as a whisper on the wind. For some moments, she contemplated whether she had really heard it. Yet, she felt uneasy about bringing him to consciousness.

"What is *wrong* with him?" Briar questioned fretfully.

Jaela shook her head to convey that nothing was wrong. She ran her thumb along his brow in contemplation, smoothing the wild path the tiny hairs had made. It seemed certain now that her qualms were correct. This was not an ordinary slumber. Further healing was required. There may be injuries they could not see. Whatever the reason, she must trust him to the Great One.

CHAPTER 15

"You cannot be serious!" Briar thundered at Farrow, hands clenched into fists at her sides. "We have dragged my brother's lazing rear about for *days*. It is the best we can do. And you just want to *bail?*"

"We will not make it in time if we maintain this pace," he returned evenly. "I cannot sacrifice Blooms for the sake of going down with the Deerskin boat."

"Except that *I* was chosen to deliver the recompense *with* you," she reminded. "What happens when you show up alone?"

His breathing slowed as he considered. His eyes found Elaine. "Will I be alone?"

Elaine pressed her lips together. She had done more than her fair share of hauling Rowan about on the makeshift cot. No matter how he was jostled, Rowan's slumber persisted and the group's unease increased. How long could he survive without sustenance? They had poured water down his throat but were never certain just how much was ingested as a deal of it spilled down his chin.

"He could wake up any day now..." Elaine began pensively.

Jaela had days ago become impressed by the girl's loyalty to the entire group—not just Farrow. She was as concerned as Briar and Jaela for Rowan's sake. Jaela often wondered if perhaps she felt more for him than she let on.

"By then, it will be too late," Farrow reminded. "We have lost too much time."

"Perhaps if *you* had helped drag him—" Briar began angrily.

"Farrow is right," Elaine admitted with the drooping of her shoulders. "I hope Rowan awakens soon, Briar. But we have no way of knowing if or when. I understand Jaela did all she could, but... it clearly was not enough."

"Please," Briar began in desperation, "Elaine, Farrow... I was selected as your tribe's champion. I cannot say why. But I *do* imagine that replacing a champion is out of the question... else why should there be a Selection Ceremony? Let me do this with you."

"Come with us," Farrow challenged.

Her mouth fell open. "I-I cannot just *leave* him—"

"She can remain with him." He gestured to Jaela. "She was selected as his fellow champion. Despite personal ties, *your* duty is to Blooms."

"But..." Briar searched for an argument, "Jaela cannot drag him alone. What about the recompense of *my* tribe?"

"That is Jaela's concern—not yours. As you said, we must trust the selection."

Briar shook her head with adamance. "Look, delivering a rec-ompense has been my dream for as long as I can remember. But I will not leave my own brother behind."

"You said yourself you were not even supposed to accompany them," Elaine put in. "Why not entrust them to whatever path the Creator has set?"

Briar's eyes narrowed. "You do realize my brother fancies you, right? He has never fancied anyone. And you would just leave him to the mercies of a lone girl?"

"A powerful one," Farrow reminded. "He remains alive be-cause of her. They do not need you. *We* do."

Jaela fumed inwardly. She had been angry enough that Farrow wished to part ways, but that he would so selfishly attempt to take Briar with him was going too far. She could not handle hauling Rowan on her own.

Unexpectedly, Briar met her eyes. "He *is* right..." she admitted shamefacedly. "They need me. And you are powerful. He may awake tonight or tomorrow and then you can catch up with us."

Jaela's eyes widened in response. They would not *truly* leave her alone to care for Rowan's large unconscious form? She dreaded what it might cost the tribe. She feared for Rowan.

"I am sorry..." Briar whispered. Kneeling beside her brother, she spoke it again. She returned to her feet with confidence. "I *will* see you again, Jaela. All will be well... I promise."

Elaine nodded an apology to Jaela as she followed after the others. Jaela's mouth fell open as she watched them go. She could not believe it. She had been abandoned. *Rowan* had been abandoned. By his own sister. Jaela was certain he would *never* do such a thing to her, even if it cost him ten tribes.

Lost for anything else to do, she grasped at Rowan's cot and heaved for all she was worth. If she could manage to cover some of the space between them, they could more easily catch up when Rowan awoke... if he *ever* awoke.

As the sun fell lower in the sky, her faith that he would do so dwindled considerably—as did every bit of strength she could muster. She had never been a strong girl and Rowan was a hefty load. Still, she continued, biting her lip with determination. If she simply did not stop, did not give up, all would be well. But she soon learned that sheer stubbornness did not carry one like a pair of wings. With trembling body, she eventually collapsed upon the path.

A tear streamed down her cheek. What a heroine she made! Even after all she had done in an attempt to save Rowan those nights ago, she was *still* useless.

And yet, when she awoke the following morning to find both Rowan and herself safe and whole, she persisted. With fresh vigor, she configured an improved method of hauling her burden. She covered more ground until her strength gave out again. At noon, she took careful measures to see that Rowan ingested water.

It was a peculiar position to be placed in—spoon-feeding someone like Rowan of Deerskin, dragging his all but deceased corpse about like a giant infant. Anyone would have expected their positions would be reversed. Yet, here she had saved him from none other than malevolent daemon sprites.

This sent her to questioning where their adversaries had been of late. They had not received another visit since the evening Rowan had been placed in his current state. She wondered if she had proved too much for them or if, impossibly, they had actually obeyed her command. With bitterness, she giggled at the thought before drawing to her feet. Fighting against the strain in her calves, she straightened her legs long enough to collapse. For the first time in her life, she had pressed herself to her limit.

Engulfed by a wave of astringent hopelessness, she dropped beside Rowan in order to lean back against a broad tree. As she gathered his head into her lap for a semblance of company, she wondered if this was the only means she had left of caring for him. Foreboding trembled through her. What would she do if he did not rouse? Would she one day face the same question Briar had? Would she leave him unguarded in the forest where daemonkind lurked in order to deliver the recompense of a tribe she did not love? But there was Mother...

It was pitch black when next she awoke. A night owl hooted overhead. She was certain it was what had wakened her. She had neglected to feed both herself and Rowan. Already, she was failing. Feeling the chill of the evening, she reached for a blanket to cover Rowan. Softly, she breathed her flame over him until he was no longer cool to the touch. As she felt around for supplies to appease her grumbling stomach, she realized Briar had left her supply pack fastened to the cot. This had been of a purpose, she was certain. An apology.

A shiver ran through her flesh as she perceived the howling of a wolf. They had heard them through the evenings, but she had trusted to the skills of those with her. Though she had bested creatures of the Nethers, she was uncertain what she could do against a natural creature. She pulled the blanket more tightly about Rowan.

"HS..." she whispered. "Are you here?"

As with Rowan's slumbering form, no response followed.

"HS, we need you," she sniveled. *"I* need you. Please, show yourself."

Not but a warm breeze in the midst of the cool night was offered in reply. Once again, she felt tears on her cheeks. Realizing they were splashing upon Rowan's face, she used his blanket to clear them away. Before long, she noted her hand brushing through his hair again. She had done it often over the days he had slumbered. It was an awkward kind of comfort. But as always, she stopped herself. It was too intimate a gesture for what they were to one another.

Yet, in her heart, she felt nearer him than he could her. He had shown her kindness even before witnessing her capabilities. More significantly, his cries the evening of the attack had done something to her heart, causing it to constrict whenever she replayed them in memory. The serenity of his face since then had endeared him to her. Even if he could not consider her a friend, he was hers. She had come to care too deeply for his wellbeing for it to be otherwise.

Come morning, she found she had slept again. It had not been her intention. She was their only means of protection, as backwards as that sounded in her mind. She looked down at Rowan's head still resting upon her leg. He slept on.

"Oh, *Rowan,* please wake up!" she urged without thinking. She had often recalled the warning that had sounded on the breeze that time ago, but it had become like a dream. So, she urged on. "You *have* to be all right. You have to *live*... Please." She watched as his nostrils imbibed the flame of her plea.

The snap of a branch resonated through the woods. Her eyes flew in that direction. A large shrub yet danced. With all her heart, she prayed it was Briar having returned after all.

In the next moment, a human cry pierced the air and four men charged into her path. She bounded to her feet, arms flying up as if to obstruct them, whomever they were—a nearby clan, she supposed. Opening her mouth, she was uncertain of what to do, what to speak. She awaited an impulse that did not arise. With a shriek, she was seized from behind. A hand settled tightly over her mouth. Another choked her about the throat.

Hot breath met her ear as a voice hissed, "Not so fast, *fire-tongue.* They warned us about you. He demands your incarceration at all costs."

Jaela could not catch her breath. Her vision darkened. She could not say what these people would do or what they wanted.

All she could surmise was that "they" were daemonkind and these men were in cahoots with them.

As suddenly as she had been apprehended, she was dropped. Free to gasp for breath, it was all she could do to fill her lungs as she bowed over the turf. Absently, she perceived cries and grunts as warfare took place around her. It seemed ages this went on—a battle she had no strength to observe as she returned from the brink of collapse. By the time all was quiet, she remained where she knelt, too terrified to lift her head and discover her fate.

When a hand touched her hair, she flung herself away, working to regain her legs.

"It is *me*, Jaela!"

She froze, falling back upon her rear in wonderment.

Rowan knelt beside her. "Are you all right? Did they harm you?"

She shook her head, though as yet she was unsure. She simply relished the relief that washed over her at finding him conscious, alive and moving about as if he had not been down a day in his life.

A smirk overspread his face at her evident pleasure. "I am all right, thanks to you," he said with a conspiratorial nod. "And I will find a way to thank you in time, believe me. For now, where are Briar and the others? They should not have left you unprotected with me sleeping the morning away."

Jaela's eyes went wide. How could she tell him... literally? She shook her head.

"You do not know?" he questioned.

She hesitated, meeting his eyes, willing him to read her mind.

"Are they nearby?" he tried.

Though she could not really be certain how far they had gone, she shook her head. She knew no other way to convey what had occurred.

"Are they... hunting fresh game?"

She shook her head again.

His head bobbed to the side as he considered her. "Do you expect them back soon, Jaela?"

Tears pricked her eyes as she shut them and shook her head with vehemence.

He fell back on his haunches. "I do not understand..." The tear that dropped down her face seemed to clue him in. He sat forward, placing hands on her shoulders. "Jaela... they did not leave us behind?"

She nodded, refusing to meet his eye. It would be nothing to him that those from Blooms abandoned him. But his own sister...

He fell back again. "H-how long have I been out?"

She held up her fingers to denote the nights.

Again, he sat forward. "You cannot be serious! *Eight,* Jaela? Are you jesting?"

She shook her head.

He ran a hand through his hair. "We have lost *eight* days?" He searched the terrain. "But we have moved?"

She pointed to the cot upon which they had dragged him.

His brows flew up. "Then why did the others leave you?"

Her own flew up at his use of "you" rather than "us." Had he simply not put everything together or was his concern chiefly for her?

"It was too slow, I wager..." he guessed.

She nodded.

Swiftly, almost desperately, he pulled the map from his pack and sat down beside her. "Show me. Show me where we are."

Her eyes fell upon the last place Briar had pointed out to her. She followed the path suggested by Deerskin until she could deduce their location. Farrow had been right. They had not covered much ground. She pointed.

Rowan crumpled the map in his hand, grasping his hair with the other. "We will not make it," he said disbelievingly. "No wonder they left." He fell into silence for a time before his gaze returned to her. "It was harsh to leave you alone with me. I might not have proved any protection for you and they knew that. Although, I suppose *you* were left to protect *me* after..." He swallowed. "I imagine you doubted I would ever wake up..." His eyes inspected her. "Why did you stay with me?"

Jaela knew not how to respond. She was not even certain herself. She simply knew she could never have done what Briar had, not even for the sake of the tribe. She had discovered that sometime in the night. The "why" escaped her until she returned his gaze. Her eyes drifted to his brows and then his hair that glistened from her ceaseless touch over the last days. Once again, his agonized cries sounded in her mind and her heart contracted. She did not wish to determine what it meant, but it came to her in any case.

Squeezing his hand before drawing to her feet, she wandered to their supplies in search of waterskins. She had heard the trickling of a stream in the night. He would need water. Food, too. Surely, he was famished.

It wasn't until she knelt beside the stream that deep trepidation gripped her. She dropped the waterskin, proceeding to scramble into the water after it. Even when she had it in her clutches, she remained where she knelt in the stream. A panicked whooshing filled her ears. It could *not* be so. And perhaps it was not. How she hoped it was not. Still, it chafed her nerves. She searched her soul, her memories, in search of the truth. Was she... had she begun to... to fall for Rowan?

She marched from the water with a mind to return to the campsite in flight of the question before she recalled *he* would be there. With exasperation, she planted herself beside the brook. Wrapping her arms about her legs, she hugged them close as she contemplated her improbable yet likely discovery.

Rowan watched Jaela's retreating frame with measures of admiration and shame. Not only had her despised tongue saved his life, she had remained loyal to him even when his own sister had felt it necessary to continue on. It must have felt an unfeasible task, lingering with one who had not known consciousness for days. He recalled, too, those initial nights in which Jaela had gone without sleep. Attempts on their camp had occurred before he was ever aware. She had tried to tell him.

Now, he was faced with a conundrum. He owed this girl. He owed her his life. Yet, since that day she had gained her strange speech and he the perception of it, he had robbed her. Though unknowingly, she had repaid duplicity with devotion.

What could he do now? He ought to confess all upon her return with the waterskins. Someone to translate her words, or to simply talk with, would be a blessing. Not enough to repay his debt but a start. But something in him knew he would not do it. And why? Was he still fearful of what others would think? He shook his head. They were beyond that now. Then... could it be he feared the pain it would cause her to learn of his years of betrayal? He shook his head. That was a factor, but he had not yet reached the truth.

He released a long breath, crushing a daisy underfoot. The fact was, despite what everyone thought, what *Jaela* thought... Rowan of Deerskin, son of Bowan the Champion, was a coward. For so long he had harbored this secret out of fear of humiliation. Now, he dreaded the concept of admitting his smallness, his shortcoming, his *cruelty* even, to one who had been so good to him.

He fell back against the tree beside which their supplies rested, wrestling with a longing to tell her the truth and the impossibility of it. He knew himself. The son of Bowan had never been one to relay his faults to others. He hid them, he ran from them and, if possible, he suppressed them.

But what did it matter anymore? They had failed to deliver the recompense on time, or soon would. The Tribe of Deerskin was in for ruin. They were *all* goners. It was said few ever escaped the fate of an accursed clan. Those of the Nethers hunted out their rightful prey until everyone was finished.

Clenching hands into fists, he glared down at them. He had once believed them so capable of this quest. Nay, he had *gloried* in the challenge and in the praises that would be sung over his outstanding success. He was supposed to have been a hero. But at his first test of strength, he had proved feral as a newborn deer. It had taken the skinny, scorned girl of his tribe to save his life. And though he had just managed to rescue her from whatever tribe had dared break the amity decree of the recompense, he yet failed to salvage Deerskin.

Feverishly, he grasped the map, smoothing it out on the ground before him. His eyes traversed its paths until he blinked down at it with something like dawning hope. There *was* a way, or there might be. It was the path that had been marked as *Forbidden Pass*. Under no circumstances, it expressed in small script, should they venture that way. He chuckled bitterly at the thought. If he died in the process, all he wanted now was to save his people. Though it was a long shot, this *could* be the key.

But *why* were they forbidden from taking it? Was it so precarious that it was hopeless to escape from? What could be worse than the fate they faced if they did not try? He stood to his feet. Where was Jaela? It seemed an age since she had wandered off. In fear and trembling, he followed her trail, fearful of finding her wounded or missing altogether. Perhaps she had left him, too. It wasn't as if they had any reason to stick together anymore. She must think they had failed as well.

With a wash of relief, he found her sitting leisurely beside the brook. She leaped in fright of his sudden appearance at her side, looking up at him with large, almost guilt-filled eyes. He seemed always to be startling her with his silent tread.

"I believe I have found a way," he spoke bluntly. Thrusting the map into her hands, he pointed. "You remember this path from the first day we set out? I suggested taking it when I thought myself invulnerable." Inwardly, he scoffed at himself. "But... it is our only option now. It is by far the shortest path into the Nethers."

He watched as her eyes fell upon the name of the pass once again. Pressing his lips together, he let her take it in. He remembered now that she had not been eager to follow it. "It is up to you," he continued. "I do not know what lies there... but it is something the clans have deemed unthinkable to face. Still, we have lost *everything* if we do not try."

Her silence spoke volumes, so he felt. And now he realized that what he asked, after everything she had done for him, was pitiless. With her gift, there might still be some chance in the world for her. Though the tribe who had long rejected her would perish, she might survive. He could not take that from her.

Seizing the map, he mumbled, "I am sorry I mentioned it. It is not feasible. You have seen too much trouble and... you would be fine if—"

Her eyes enlarged as she faced him. Drawing swiftly to her feet, she stomped as she pointed at the map.

He glanced down at it as if it possessed an answer. Perhaps it did. "You... wish to try it?"

Fervently, she nodded, eyes burning with offense—pain even.

He leaped to his own feet, dropping the map. "I did not mean... I do not think you a *coward,* Jaela. I just... I feel you deserve the chance you would have on your own. I did not consider what I might be asking—"

A measure of fire receded from her eyes, but still she pointed to the map on the ground. To his astonishment, she even spoke.

"We must."

He blinked back at her. Did she expect him to understand? Did she *know?* Or did she feel so strongly about it that she could not keep silent?

"Are you sure?" he chanced, hoping she would assume he only guessed at her words. But now he had convinced her, he almost regretted it for her sake. Even so, they were the chosen champions of Deerskin. They owed them their all.

She nodded, fire returning to her eyes.

"Very well," he answered with a hint of amusement. She had never been so vexed with him before. "But... *please* know that I do not doubt your courage. I saw you in action, after all."

Her eyes flew to his as if searching. For what, he could only guess.

"I saw some of it—what you did to those creatures. And I experienced a miracle by your language. I no longer see you as I did before. I thought myself your protector, but it was you who protected all of us. I was very, *very* wrong. And..." Here, his voice cracked with either emotion or guilt—he could not just say. "I am *sorry*... for everything you have endured since coming into your amazing gift."

Her eyes widened in bewilderment. It hit him. He had deemed a gift what their tribe regarded as a curse. Maybe that was world-changing. "I will tell them all..." he assured, "should we make it back. I will tell them how wrong they have been. They will know you for what you truly are."

He was touched by the tears that rimmed her eyes. She turned away, returning her gaze to the stream. He allowed her a moment. He could not imagine what it was like to be scorned the whole of one's life and then finally gain something of the recognition due. He had always received respect he did not rightfully deserve. In frustration, he lifted the map from the ground, absently smoothing it before folding it into neatness.

"What did the others think?" he spoke hoarsely after some moments. "What did they make of your ability to best the dark creatures?"

To his surprise, she turned to shake her head, pointing to her eyes and shaking her head again.

"They... did not see them?"

She nodded.

"But I saw Briar and Farrow wake up just as the last of those things retreated. How did they not see?"

She raised her brows as if this was fresh news. Finally, she pointed to her eyes once again, along with the shaking of her head. They *could* not see them, she intimated. He now recalled the beasts' surprise at his ability to perceive their presence.

Her eyes alit on him as what he conjectured to be the same question came to each of their minds. Why could they see what others could not? He dropped his gaze at recognition of the likeliest answer. They had been affected by the same strange being ten years prior. He longed to ask her who it was, but that was a satchel of worms through which he was not prepared to wade.

CHAPTER 16

Jaela was grateful for the instant cure. Rowan having supposed she would turn her back on the tribe in order to protect herself reminded her of what she was in his eyes. Perhaps his estimation had risen to an extent, but she was still an inhuman, wild thing—like a pathetic animal of the forest. Her heart ceased its dance of involuntary sentimental ideals. She was *free*.

And what was there to love about Rowan anyway? Yes, he was fine-looking, strong, capable and he had shown her consideration. But did he possess attributes she would wish for in someone she loved? After a moment, she realized she had never contemplated what such characteristics would be. She had never expected the chance to care for someone in that way. Nothing had altered in that arena. Therefore, she determined to put it from her mind and be grateful she was no longer in danger of falling for Rowan of Deerskin.

As they gathered up their supply packs, Rowan noticed the extra. "Did Briar forget this?"

She nodded.

He stared at it. "I do not care for that. She is entirely at their mercy for supplies." After some moments' thought, he added, "She left it as an apology, did she not?"

A shrug was her answer.

"Sheesh, *Briar*, do you not realize I just want you safe?" he murmured into the treetops.

Jaela considered this. She had been hurt and despondent that Briar, of all people, had abandoned her own brother. Rowan in no way shared these feelings. He seemed to understand the choice she had made and longed more for his sister's wellbeing than his own. Was this a side to him that he had always maintained or was their journey changing him as it was her?

For the remainder of the morning, they traveled toward the Forbidden Pass, each harboring secret thoughts. Though Jaela was willing to face what danger she must to save her tribe—specifically, her mother—her mind roved for some peril that could be worse than the Nethers, the underworld of the dead. They were *required* to enter that frightening realm, yet forbidden from this pass... That left a deal of room for consideration when one was marching toward it.

"So..." Rowan began, breaking the silence, "you *really* dragged me for days—you and the others, I gather?"

A gleam appeared in her eyes for answer. It had not been easy, but they had managed.

He shook his head. "That is impressive. I am no small sack of potatoes. And I am surprised Farrow agreed to the slower pace."

She raised a brow at him.

"Ah. He is the reason they left us behind."

She nodded.

"Well, thank you... again," he continued, "for staying with me. Would not have felt very nice awakening to find myself alone, at best. I much preferred springing up to defend a damsel in distress... especially when I was the damsel last time I saw your face."

Jaela observed something in his eyes that made her look away: admiration... Admiration for what she had done for him that night?

"And we are fortunate you did your work so well," he continued soberly. "That was a lot of people to send for just one girl and a sleeping huntsman..." His eyes narrowed as he drew her gaze to his own. "It sounded to me as if they were after you specifically... Would that have something to do with your gift or did you delve up other enemies while I was sleeping?"

Jaela was once again astonished by his use of the term "gift." At the same time, she scarcely recalled what their attackers had said—only that they were fellow clansmen and she had felt herself helpless against them. Had daemons sent them because they knew her defenses failed when it came to people? She now recalled that the tribesmen had said "he" wanted her at all costs. A shiver sent trembles through her as she questioned who "he" could be.

"We must be on our guard at all times," Rowan murmured upon witnessing her reaction. He proceeded to notch an arrow in his bow. "But do not forget what you did for me. At this rate,

I begin to wonder what you are *not* capable of with that superior tongue."

Jaela eyed him sidelong, wondering if she was perhaps not so safe from her heart-stirrings as she had hoped. It did not help that he was treating her like someone of consequence. And... he was Rowan.

That evening, they encamped upon a small mountain. The lack of tree coverage made Jaela feel vulnerable. She was relieved when Rowan suggested they neglect a fire. Even so, it was a chilly night. If she had been able to voice her opinion, they would have stopped at the base of the mountain, where they might have enjoyed the tree coverage as well as a fire. But by the way Rowan had proceeded the remainder of the day, she doubted he would have allowed a fire in any case. He was spooked and, therefore, determined to cover as much ground as possible. Come morning, they would start into the Forbidden Pass below. So, she wrapped herself tightly in her bedroll and relented to rest.

"Jaela."

She bolted upright at the whisper.

"Quiet," Rowan urged.

"What is it?" she whispered without thinking.

"We are not alone," he answered.

A shiver flushed through her.

"I am going 'hunting' and wanted you to be aware."

He started off, dagger in hand. A bow would be useless under the light of a halfmoon. Jaela wished she had followed after him. She felt herself a sitting duck where she was. It seemed an age she sat there alone, listening for movements that never came. What if something had happened to Rowan?

"I could use some light," a voice spoke into the darkness.

Jaela's scream sent a torrent of flame over none other than Briar.

The two sat in silence for some moments before Briar spoke quietly, "I am *so* glad I am not a pile of ashes right now."

"Jaela?!" Rowan boomed as his feet stamped across the rocky mountaintop. He sounded as if he would tear her would-be attacker to pieces given the chance.

"Celestial twilight, big brother!" Briar shouted back.

Jaela took the initiative to relight the torch they had used to climb the foothills in the dim twilight, shining it squarely between the siblings. The two stood staring at one another—Rowan with astonishment, Briar evidently amused.

"You did not *really* believe I had ditched you, did you?" Briar asked. "I left my pack and everything. Farrow was decidedly unhappy about that."

Rowan was speechless some moments before wrapping his arms tightly around her. "I understood why you had gone... or thought I did," he said. "But I am relieved to have you safe with me." Suddenly, he pulled back. "But why did you leave then?"

With a half-smile, she reached into her pocket to pull out a small brown satchel. "The recompense for Blooms."

"Briar..." Rowan began in disbelief, "you *stole* their recompense? They are counting on you!"

"Certainly. But I was of no mind to forsake my sleeping beauty of a brother in the woods, let alone his guardian angel." She cast Jaela a nod. "This girl and I spent too many days dragging your lazy behind around to just give up on you. Still... I wanted to fulfill my duty as champion, so I needed these." She tossed the satchel into the air before restoring it to her pocket.

Rowan shook his head as if uncertain what to make of her. Jaela couldn't help grinning. Perhaps it would not appear an honorable choice to someone from Blooms, but it was *very* Briar. When she wanted her way, she got it.

"Hey, Farrow should not have been so determined to ditch you," Briar defended. "And I reckon the rubies will be just as well off with us as with them. Better even. There are three of us and we have her." She pointed to Jaela.

"Well... I am grateful to have you in my care again," Rowan returned with a sigh.

"Your care? I am *sorry*... Who was the one drip-feeding you liquids for half a fortnight?" She turned to Jaela for support. "It felt like we were raising a newborn infant who never ate nor wakened. It was a delicate business."

If Jaela did not know any better, she would say Rowan was blushing under the torchlight.

"I hope things will be different for the remainder," he answered. "We are better aware of what we face now."

Briar dug her boot into the rocky ground as if frustrated. "About that, what *are* we facing? What *happened* to you?"

"Daemons." Rowan exchanged a glance with Jaela to verify his conjecture.

She nodded her agreement.

"Daemons..." Briar repeated, "outside of their realm. That does not bode well, concerning all we have heard."

"They tried to kill me," Rowan agreed with a nod. "And, unless I am mistaken, they want Jaela."

The two looked upon Jaela, to which she merely widened her eyes. She wasn't accustomed to so much attention.

"All right, then," Briar replied, "She is our prize. Inasmuch as she has cared for you, we must protect her."

Rowan released a sort of grumbling laugh. *"She* was the one who bested them."

Briar looked upon Jaela with a raised brow. *"Really?* Is our little sparrow proving herself more lioness than we estimated? I would like to see you in action, Jaela of Deerskin." She returned her attention to her brother. "We never saw any daemons, you know. Just Jaela breathing fire everywhere."

He nodded. "Only Jaela and I could see them."

"And why would that be?"

"...We are not certain."

"All right... Uh, last question: what are we doing *here?* It took me forever to pick out your trail or I would likely have found you this morning. I thought this path was to be avoided like the plague?"

"It is the fastest route. I cannot see another way of making it in time."

"I began to determine that when I went with the others. It was cutting it close by the route they took. But we cannot really consider taking this one, can we?"

"And why not?" His hands went to his hips.

She sputtered. "Because it is apparently so perilous that we are not even supposed to consider it."

"What is the danger?"

"I... I do not know." She reached for her map. "It does not say."

"Exactly. It is the swiftest route and what could be worse than the Nethers?"

"That *is* a question..."

"How were you expecting to make it in time anyway?"

"That was not a question," she answered boldly. "I would learn to fly if I had to."

As suddenly as a flash of lightning, the sky lit up around them. Jaela clutched her bedroll as the three peered up in breathless wonder. The Celestial Event was making its first appearance, signaling the beginning of the Celestial Festivities. Back home, they were gathered about fires in the familiar wood, feasting on delicacies while enjoying dancing and music that had been prepared long before time. But here they stood upon a clear mountaintop, not a thing between them and the spectacle.

"I have never seen it like this," Briar whispered as florescent blue and green danced across the sky.

"Me neither," Rowan murmured.

Problem was, the phenomena proved they really were cutting it close to the delivery date of the recompense. Some would likely have already arrived and departed from the Nethers. The champions who lived nearest were probably feasting with their home clans. Yet, here they were with the best view one could ask for. It was true they had not yet succeeded, nor were they home to enjoy the festivities. But Jaela felt this vantage felt akin with peeking into the glory of another realm—perhaps the Great One's own kingdom.

The siblings took a seat on either side of Jaela as they witnessed the manifestation. Jaela was almost more awed by the company she kept, that they should care to enjoy the spectacle *with* her instead of apart from her. Could it be... they were becoming friends? Or, should they return in one piece, would everything go back to the way it was? She shook her head. It did no good to dwell on the future. She had no control over that. For the present, she was at her leisure.

"What is the matter?" Rowan whispered in response to her headshake.

She shook her head again, pointing up at the sky. She wouldn't have explained the truth if she could.

"It looks like your fire," he commented wistfully.

"It really does," Briar added excitedly. "Show us. Say something!"

Jaela shook her head. She did not speak for show. The last time she had, Old Willow had lost a couple decades of age.

"Oh, come on!" Briar pressed. "Tell us how it felt getting stuck dragging Rowan around all that time." She chuckled. "It is not as if we will understand you."

Jaela blushed at the thought, grateful they had snuffed the torch. She found herself once again tempted to do as bid. This was something like a dream, having companions such as these who actually wished her to speak. "It was..." She searched for the truth. "...worth it."

"See?" Briar returned with eagerness. "It really does look like the sky. How beautiful!"

To Jaela's bewilderment, Rowan spoke no more. He enjoyed the remainder in silence until it was considered judicious to turn in for the evening. They were due for an early morning's breakfast before entering the pass

Jaela tossed with the voice that pursued her in the night. She knew that sound like the back of her hand but could not seem to make out his words. They echoed off the caverns of her mind, intermingled with the sounds of the evening that pricked her consciousness. Of a sudden, she was soaring over mountains, planes and oceans, then through a blinding light in the sky that carried her among the stars. Finally, she floated over a distant sphere of green, blue and white.

"This is planet Earth," HS informed.

Upon his word, she was plummeting toward it. In a blurred haze, she soon observed a man among a grove of trees. He knelt upon the ground, crying out to the stars.

"He calls to his father," HS explained with somberness, "the Great One."

Jaela scarcely had time to take in what this could mean when she experienced flashes of the man laying hands upon people to see them healed. Like her, he spoke to daemons and they fled. Wherever he went, people *awoke* and there was fullness of joy. They loved him and they followed his paths. They could not help themselves—he was magnetic. Even Jaela wished to follow but could not seem to move her appendages.

She remained in the garden where he sobbed. His sweat mingled with blood revealed foreboding as she had never thought to witness. He pled with his father for escape. Whatever lay in his future was something even this phenomenal person dreaded. She did not know a soul could endure such anguish. Yet... in the end, his tears ceased. He washed the bloody sweat from his face and stood resolutely upon his feet.

As if on cue, another man approached with arms outstretched. Would he comfort him? Yes, he kissed him upon the cheek. Jaela sighed with relief.

"He is betrayed, Jaela," HS echoed into her mind as if he would weep himself.

It was then she understood what she had seen drip from the kiss—poison. He would die. Something in her bawled against it. She heaved with the wrongness of it. Though her glimpse of him had been momentary and minute, she was endeared to him. He was familiar. HS's words struck her. This was the son of her *God*. And he would die?

"The Anointed One is betrayed," HS spoke again, "but this is only the beginning." His tone exchanged solemnity for an anticipation that made his heart audibly pound into her ears.

"The verdict is in. I have loved you with an everlasting love. Your recompense shall be paid in full, forevermore."

CHAPTER 17

ROWAN OPTED TO KEEP the night watch. It was imperative Jaela catch up on sleep. He was of no mind to entrust it to Briar. Who knew how little rest Jaela had managed when they were alone, not to mention beforehand? She would require all the strength she could garner for whatever they were to face on the morrow.

He recalled the way her fire had mingled with the hues of the Celestial Spectacle. Releasing a breath, he could not help feeling it had been the finest moment of the journey. After all, his sister had returned for him, Jaela had never left his side and the view from the mountaintop had been breathtaking. He would not trade his current lot for the world.

It startled him how different he felt, as if he possessed a whole new outlook. It was as if everything had changed over the course of a really long nap. Even his position in this smaller group was altered. He was no longer their chief means of protection. Much as he wanted to be, he wasn't the hero.

Jaela was.

And they were only just coming to know her capabilities. What of her hopes and dreams, her heartsong, as the clans put it? Due to her strange speech, they might never know. He, however, could learn more than others... such as her response to Briar's question—that dragging and nursing him had been "worth it." What did it mean? And... was it true?

Jaela's abilities alone revealed she had been grossly underestimated. It was not just. And was it his fault? He might have explained her to their people. They could have revered her. She would not have been the "wild thing." Indeed, he began to feel that she was more composed than he was. Thus far, she had taken everything in stride.

Though he had become the damsel in distress when it mattered most, he continued to feel burdened with a need to protect his comrades. Problem was, he now understood how ill-equipped he was. It made the burden all the heavier as he sat up in the long hours of the night. It was impossible to feel safe.

As sunrise dawned in tender hues, Jaela whimpered softly, sending flame into the atmosphere. Her face constricted as Rowan knelt beside her in search of some unseen danger. Discovering no sprites about, he concluded it was a customary nightmare. He arose to leave when she moaned again. Should he wake her? His eyes sought the horizon. They must move on soon in any case.

"Jaela.... Jaela, wake up," he murmured with a gentle shake.

Though she did not open her eyes, her even breathing proved she was conscious.

"Is all well?" he inquired.

"Bad... dream," she murmured as if still held by it.

"It is over now," he soothed, "and it was but a dream."

Her eyes shot open, locking on him. "It was *not* just a dream. He has been betrayed!" A tear streamed down her temple.

"Who?" he questioned. Among the clans, dreams were considered to mean something.

Without warning, Briar shot up in her bedroll, eyes fixed on her elder brother. "Rowan... how do you know what she speaks?"

His mouth fell open as he gazed back. A wave of nausea coursed through him. He had not realized what he was doing.

"Did something change while I was away?" she pressed.

Jaela sat up, eyes intent and questioning. Rowan's gaze shot to hers a moment... or what was meant to be a moment. He was pinned by her silent question until his own eyes answered.

"How?" Jaela probed with eyes narrowed in confusion.

Painfully, Rowan drew to his feet. He turned his back to them as his hands were clasped behind his back. This was his moment—the moment he must face what he had done. He must face his fear. He turned back to Jaela.

"I followed you that day... the day your father's cruelty sent you to the mercies of the forest."

Jaela's eyes were large and searching.

"I wanted to make certain you were all right. But... that thing—that strange being—beat me to it. I was there when he spoke to you, touched your head... and altered you." He swallowed as her eyes danced with tears. "I... fell to my back under its power and was held there. Once free, I ran without thinking. I was frightened. I did not think to make certain you were all right until after...

"Then, they said you could not speak for grief. I thought perhaps you *had* loved your father that much, despite his brutality. But, eventually, they said you had lost your senses and I believed that, too... until I overheard you, one day, in your hollow tree. For a long time, I was not certain why others could not perceive what you spoke, why sometimes it seemed even you could not grasp your articulations. But, through dreams, I realized..."

Here, his voice broke. This had been his deepest secret for years. He had pledged never to tell it. Now, he was admitting his coldness to the very one who would feel it most, to one who had stayed with him in his unending slumber when none else had, to one who had dragged him and nursed him and called the trouble worth it. But face her, he must, or live forever the coward.

"Through dreams, I realized you were not the only one altered that day. The being's power struck me, too, and... I received the ability to understand your speech."

Jaela's eyes glittered in shock some moments before dropping to her hands in her lap. It was as if she did not know how to look at him or what to make of his confession.

Briar was not so short of tongue. *"Hold* on," she voiced like the bear to which she was often compared. "You have understood her all along, this *whole* journey—long before that even? You could have made her understood to everyone and you chose not to. *Why*, Rowan?"

"I..." He swallowed. "I was a coward... of the lowest kind. I feared... well, we all know how she was viewed. I was a selfish boy. I did not wish to go down with her ship. I feared the rejection she endured and... I just wanted to be normal."

"All right," Briar replied with a nod, "I can see that, as a *boy*, it would be difficult. But you are a man now. And you let us think the whole of our travels that no one could translate for her. She could have warned us about the daemons and you might not have been knocked out for half a fortnight. We would not have had to take the Forbidden Pass. Why did you not *say* something?"

He gazed back at his sister as she trembled with rage. He had not realized she cared so much for Jaela. Or perhaps she was enraged at learning he was not who everyone thought he was, that he was not a truthteller and he was not fearless.

"You could have at *least* told our village what happened to her in the forest!" Briar cried again.

Jaela flew to her feet. She did not meet his eyes. Instead, she started down the mountain... the wrong side of the mountain.

"Jaela!" he tried desperately. Would she return home? Or simply disappear? He raced after her, grasping her wrist. *"Please, Jaela, I am so sorry. I should have said something... I should have told you long ago, or even yesterday. I have wronged you... and I deeply regret it."*

Her eyes were filled with fire when she turned back to look at him. For a moment, it appeared as if she would wrench herself from his grasp without a word. Then, she seemed to recall that she could speak plainly to him.

"Let me go," she said in a low voice, tight with emotion.

"But I—"

"I said *release* me!" she growled, fire blazing hot over his person.

Feeling like a fool, he released her. She stood some moments to observe every facet of his face—thinking what, he could not determine. He wished she would speak. But when she did, he wished she had not.

"Let us go on as we have after this moment, Rowan of Deerskin," she spoke bitterly. "I never wish to speak to you again." With that, she continued down the mountain.

Briar started down the opposite side. He was torn for what to do. Would Briar face the pass alone? He should not let her. But he did not wish to leave things as they were with Jaela. If she chose to disappear, it may be forever. He looked one way and then the other. Finally, he dropped upon the ground. He would do nothing. What good had he done the whole of their quest? He would sit and he would wait and if a daemon sprite came to pluck him up, he would not fight it.

Jaela smothered her sobs as she picked her way down the rocky path. She could scarcely believe this turn of events. She had feared falling for the very person who had been betraying her all along. She came to a halt as the truth washed over her again.

Rowan could *understand* her?

Rowan could understand her. And he had chosen to pretend he could not, that he knew nothing, all this time. She marched on again. How she had *ached* to be able to communicate with her people. To learn that there was such a person all this time—someone who could have translated for her at precarious moments—made her heart constrict painfully.

She hated him—hated Rowan as she had never hated in her life. Like every other girl, she had admired him. He had seemed different from all else, treating her as an equal though she was so peculiar. Discovering his secret in no way explained why this was so... except that perhaps his guilt had softened his manner.

Of a sudden, it came back to her how nice it had been to speak to him as she had awoken that morning, and receive an answer. At the time, she had not been conscious enough to realize what transpired until Briar had spoken. Now, she understood why she had felt so comforted. Back and forth communication... She had not experienced that in a long, long while—not with a human, in any case.

And she would never have it again. She had told him she wished to go on as before. And she meant it... or hoped she did. Oh, it was perplexing to wish to speak with someone more than anything, simply because she *could,* and never to speak to him again for the rest of their existences.

She raised her head as something familiar arrested her senses. The fragrance was sweet and spicy at once. What did it call to mind? The crimson roses at the garden of Blooms. To her right, she spotted a pair of shrubs, their buds beckoning in the breeze.

Tears halted as her attention was absorbed. Passing between the bushes, a sudden flash of light blinded her. In the next moment, she was sitting in the dark. Her gasp illuminated her surroundings. She gasped once more in disbelief of finding herself in her hollow tree back home. Was she dreaming? She stood to exit, to test the occurrence. All she now yearned for was to sit in her mother's arms.

"Celestial birthday greetings, Jaela."

HS was beside her.

She flung her arms about him and sobbed into his shoulder. He held her tight, caressing her back. The sensation was even sweeter than a mother's arms as serenity surged through her. With the ceasing of her tears, she released a satisfied sigh. Finally, she took in his greeting. Pulling back, she dashed the tears from her cheeks.

"It is my birthday? I had not thought of it—not since before the Selection Ceremony."

"I never forgot for a moment."

She peered about the hollow again. "Is this a gift? Did you bring me home?"

He shook his head, giving her arm a sympathetic squeeze. "Your journey is not yet over. You must know that."

With the dropping of her head, she admitted, "I suppose I do. It is just... after everything..."

"Rowan's truths?"

"If that is what you wish to call them."

"Do you regret that he can understand you?"

Fiery eyes shot to his. "Of course not. I regret that he has kept it from me all this time."

"But now that you know, you have someone to talk to. A translator will be handy."

"He is *not* my translator. He is a liar. He... he did not desire to share my lot. I suppose I cannot entirely blame him. But he left me all *alone.*"

With a nod of understanding, his eyes went to the slit of light through the hollow. "I thought an interpreter might be nice for you. I have urged him to relay his truth for years. Now that he has, I hope you will not throw it away over an offense. You know how I feel about forgiveness."

"But HS," she began through the constricting of her throat, "he does not *wish* to be my interpreter. He does not want anything to do with me. Is that not clear?"

He considered her some moments before, "I am not so sure it is. Things have changed, have they not? You showed deep loyalty when he was in his direst need. And unlike most, he apologized to you for his wrongdoing. I assure you it has eaten at him the whole of your expedition. He *is* sorrowful. He sees his wrong. He does not excuse it. Sometimes, that is the best we may expect."

Her eyes flew back and forth between his. "I do not understand the advantage of forgiveness. What good does it ever do the forgiver?"

To her surprise, he chuckled. "What would you do if I chose never to forgive your wrongdoings?"

"I... well, that is different. You are very merciful. That is your prerogative."

"I will tell you what would happen. At the completion of your life, you would spend forever in the Nethers."

Her brows rose. "But the recompense..."

"Recompense *nothing,*" he answered bitterly with the wave of his hand. "I spoke to you in your dreams. What did I say?"

Her mind raced. It felt so far away. She had all but forgotten it. "You said... my recompense was to be paid in full, forevermore. What does that mean? And since when does the Creator have a son?"

"Since about thirty-three years ago—or from before time began, if you wish to be precise. You see, the Anointed One—that is, the son of the Great One—existed from before the beginning. He was with God and... he was God."

She blinked. "God's son *is* God... And that makes sense how?"

"I am him, as well. You have never questioned that."

She sighed with frustration. "Why would you pay our recompense?"

"Why would we make mankind, my love? We wanted you. We chose you. We love you. But we desire your love in return. We want it freely. There had to be a choice."

"Seems to me we have chosen poorly. We will never be deserving of you."

He clucked at her. "Never say never, for nothing is too difficult for me and nothing impossible."

She heard his heart beat faster as a wave of something she could not explain washed over her.

"He is really going to make things better?" she questioned wistfully.

"He is going to change everything."

"When?"

Though she could not imagine why, he consulted his wrist. "I would say... it is about finished." His smoldering eyes flew to hers. "You had best hurry back to your friends. There is little time before the spectacle."

"Spectacle? We saw it last night."

"Not that one, my friend. Now, *get on.*"

In her next breath, Jaela was standing behind Rowan on the mountaintop. Her heart pounded with the things HS had claimed—with the sensation of his enthusiasm, his heartbeats. It also throbbed at the sight of Rowan's very dear form looking into the horizon as if there was nothing left to live for.

"Come on," she barked as she started down the other side of the mountain. "We must hurry."

He leaped to his feet in astonishment, watching her as she went. Wordlessly, he bent to take up their packs and follow after. At the foot of the mountain, they found Briar waiting for them.

"Have you worked things out?" she questioned. It was clear her frustration had dissipated. "It seems to me we are on a schedule."

Jaela continued without answering. HS had imparted a quickening into her spirit. For the first time on this quest, she was eager for whatever purpose he had in store. All she gathered was that this could be no ordinary recompense. If something was transpiring, she did not want to miss it.

"Well," Briar began as she caught up with her. "This is it—the pass." Warily, she looked about. "Does not look like much to me. Just a bunch of rock." She slapped the mountainous wall of the pass with her hand.

Jaela's stomach twisted. She had nearly forgotten that the route they had chosen purported unknown risk. She cast her eyes up the ridgelines to be certain no one and nothing observed them. Was that a retreating shadow? Goosebumps flooded her arms. They continued tremulously until the rocky ridges gave way to an ordinary forest. By this time, they breathed a sigh of relief.

"I gather the coast is clear," Briar said easily.

Jaela nearly nodded when laughter sounded in the distance. The three halted as they listened on. It sounded much like the Celestial Festivities of some clan.

Rowan approached with map in hand. "It says there is a tribe nearby, though I have never heard of them. The Clan of Covenants?"

"I wonder what covenants they keep," Briar commented with little interest. "Well, should we approach in hopes of fresh provisions and a safe place to rest?"

Jaela shook her head. "No time."

Briar raised her brows in consternation before looking to her brother.

"She wishes to hurry," he answered quietly, as if the very act of translating her tongue was like the turning of a knife in his gut.

Jaela started on again. She could not face him. She knew HS urged her to forgive, but how could she when the mere fact of his understanding her words pained him so? She would not speak again if she could help it.

A stifled cry escaped her as a lofty form with staff in hand stepped into her path.

"State your tribe," the man demanded without pleasantries.

CHAPTER 18

ROWAN STEPPED UP BESIDE Jaela. "What is the meaning of this?"

"Relax, young man," the stranger spoke easily. "I am of the Clan of Covenants, just yonder." He pointed. "We do not allow travelers to pass beyond our village without taking record of their status. If you will come with me, you will be well fed and clothed and may continue on your way directly."

"Thanks for the offer," Rowan replied, "but we have not got much time. We have only a couple days left to pay the recompense, as you know."

The man waved a hand. "Come with me and we will escort you to the swiftest route available. You will lose no time."

Rowan looked to the others, who both shook their heads with dissatisfaction.

"Much obliged," he answered, "but we will continue along our own path."

In a matter of moments, they were surrounded. The stranger merely smiled. "We mean you no harm whatever. On the contrary, we plan to make certain you are right in the eyes of the Creator. Come along and you will see."

Those surrounding prodded them with staffs as if they were a flock of sheep.

Rowan's mind raced for what to do. They claimed they wished only to take their status and see them summarily on their way. Perhaps they were in no danger. But if this proved untrue, he must be ready. He shot a glance at Briar to make certain she would be as well. If Jaela had been willing to meet his eyes, he might have urged her. That seemed out of the question at the moment.

His fear of danger dissipated as they entered Covenants. It was adorned with white sheaths of cloth, strands of precious pearls and numerous white flowers. It was as if it was prepared for a wedding feast. Its inhabitants frolicked about until his sister was provoked to speak.

"What goes on here, friend?" she inquired of their guide.

"Why, the Celestial Festivities are in swing. Do not they celebrate such things where you are from?"

"Sure," she answered, "but our people are not usually so... excitable. At least not until the festivities begin in the evenings."

"Ah, but we are always jovial."

"And why is that?"

"We live by the order of the River's Way. Our lifestyle is pure according to their recorded statutes. We do not even have need to send our young people into the Nethers. There is no recompense to be paid. Would not your people be as jovial if you could make such claims?"

Rowan blinked at Briar, who raised a brow in return.

"I have never heard of such living," Briar answered, "at least not without the purification of the River Lifespring."

He waved a hand. "We have no need for a spring. We live by the statutes."

"Right," she answered doubtfully.

Before long, they entered a large tent, completely adorned in white. At the far end, an elder in a single chair set like a throne awaited their approach. At the urging of the staffs, they did so.

The elder with cloudlike beard and kindly, crinkling eyes greeted them warmly, "Celestial sunrise, young folks! You are the first travelers of the recompense that we have had the pleasure of welcoming this annum. We typically have the pleasure of receiving one or two pairs each year, though there were *many* more in former days. But... you seem to be a trio. How came this to be?"

"I represent a separate tribe," Briar answered proudly.

His gaze traveled from Briar, to the two with her, and back again. "Tell me, how came you to travel together?"

Rowan stepped before his sister. It was difficult to tell what this was about. He wanted to be the one giving the answers. "This is my sister."

The elder's face relaxed into a smile. "That is *very* right and proper." He ended with a satisfied nod to the man who had guided them from the path. Then, his gaze went to Jaela. "And this is?"

"She is the other champion selected to represent my tribe," he answered. What was the use of hiding it? They were all champions. This was expected.

"I see, I see," the man answered easily. "And she is... another sister? Your wife, perhaps?"

Rowan felt his face flush somewhat, but he answered simply, "A friend."

"Ah..." the tribe leader sounded. His satisfaction had waned. "And has *she* a brother of some kind along with you?"

Rowan was taken aback. It was unusual for champions to bring siblings, to say nothing of any extra company. "Er... she has not."

The elder smirked with sympathetic remorse as he snapped his fingers. Before Rowan was aware of what transpired, he and Jaela had been seized. Briar's weapons were stripped from her, but she remained free.

"What goes on here?!" Rowan shouted as he fought his captors.

"Do not fret, young one," the elder replied as he came to his feet. "We endeavor to make you right before the Creator. It is not proper to travel with a young woman who is not of your family, nor is it respectable that she should travel with you. If it were merely you and your sister, you would be free to go as promised. But this poor girl here must be made pure. You do not desire to dishonor her, do you?"

Rowan shook his head with bewilderment over the speech. The tribes never spoke this way. "Of course I do not dishonor her. I have never touched her, if that is the inference! We were merely selected to deliver the recompense together. It is always a male and female!"

"Indeed, indeed. We have long sought to remedy the unrighteousness of that fact. And you *shall* deliver your recompense, young man. But first, it is imperative you be made right before the Creator." His eyes shot to their escort. "Serenos, see they are properly attired for the occasion." He rubbed his hands together. "We have not had such opportunity all annum and *just* in time for the Celestial Festivities. It shall be a grand ceremony!"

"What ceremony?!" Rowan questioned as he was dragged in one direction, while Jaela was taken in the other.

"Why, your wedding, young man! And what a comely wife you will have. You may thank us later."

Rowan was soon stuffed into a tent where a band of elder women greeted him.

"So, this is the fortunate groom!" the eldest spoke in welcome. Gesturing to a curtain, she continued, "You may bathe just there. Your guards will accompany you to make certain there is no tricky business. We have had escapees in past. You will find a fresh set of clothes awaiting you at the finish. From there, we ladies will apply the finishing touches. This will certainly be a day to remember!"

Without further ado, he was thrust into the bathing chamber. Turning to examine the men who stood guard, he questioned whether he could take them. It was not beyond his skill. He flew at the first, summarily knocking him unconscious. His second assailant was tossed into the steaming water while three more came for him at once. He managed to knock two off their feet with the sweep of his leg and was turning to the last when the soundest punch he had ever endured sent first stars and then darkness to his vision. Last thing he knew, he was plunged into the hot water.

⟶≫⟩ ⟨≪⟵

Jaela shivered after her warm bath. Attendants polished her skin with fresh flower petals, making her smell like the garden of Blooms. Others attended her hair. They avowed this would be the finest day of her life, while her stomach toiled with fear that Rowan might not find a way to stop the proceedings. What kind of tribe was this that forced single young people into matrimony? She was but eighteen *this* day and the tribes did not typically consider it prudent to be joined in marriage until they reached at least twenty years.

Her own mind raced for a means of escape. This was not how this day was supposed to go. By HS's urgings, they must reach the Nethers with haste. Instead, she was being primped and prodded for an unwanted marriage.

Marry Rowan? She could not under any circumstances—for her own sake, to say nothing of his. Time and again, she had heard him describe his aspirations. He did not wish to be wedded until he had made a name for himself and then only to the very finest match he could acquire under the circumstances. This was the opposite. She trembled at the thought of facing him like a nightmare in white.

"Do not be nervous, ya sweet thing," soothed the woman cleansing her hands. "Ye're young, but he seems a *fine* young man. This ceremony will purify ya. Then, you will not have to worry about ill repute among the clans."

Jaela rolled her eyes. Whether or not their traveling status was considered righteous to this tribe, it was entirely unseemly to be forced into marriage by them. After all, unions within the clans were forever. There was no going back. Though she found her stomach fluttered at the mere notion of being *honestly* wedded to Rowan, a partnership in which he was discontentedly imprisoned was worse than death. She could not do it to him. But how could she stop it?

⇒⇒⇒⇒ ⇐⇐⇐⇐

Rowan was awoken by the glaring fragrance of a garden before he realized it was himself. Glancing into a rare glass against the wall, he discovered he was all in white with his hair combed back in a way he had never seen it before. He looked agreeable. This was just how he would like to appear on his wedding day... perhaps ten years hence and to a woman of his choosing.

On an impulse, he tried the exit to find himself thrust back inside. Glancing about the walls of the tent, he observed the forms of twenty or so men standing guard around it. With a disgusted grunt, he fell back upon the ground. Something had to give...

someone must stop this. He was supposed to be protecting Jaela. Here, he could not even rescue her from himself—the person who had lied to her for the last eight years.

Running a hand through his glistening locks, he imagined what it would be like if this was not the case, if he had *chosen* Jaela. But he knew he never would. He liked Jaela. He had come to respect her. But he had planned to be wedded to someone like... well, someone like Elaine—brave, bold and beautiful.

Jaela was pretty enough, when she tried. And he had discovered her courage, along with the sheer power of her strange speech. But her lack of usual dialogue was a drawback. He could befriend someone like her, but to have her for a *wife?*

His mind roved over the course of their journey. All along, he had been burdened to care for her as a helpless damsel. But he had only helped her the one time. She, on the other hand, had remained by his side for days on end while he was more vulnerable than he had ever been in his life. Even Briar had left him, if only for a time. Yet, anything might have happened in that stretch. Jaela had *stayed.*

And she had thought him worth the trouble.

He sat up straight as it occurred to him that he could do worse. True, his boyhood had been filled with dreams of glory and grandeur, including the status of his future spouse. But Jaela *was* something of a treasure. She had sent a daemonic scourge to flight, after all. Had Elaine ever managed such a thing?

As if led by an unseen force, he recalled how Jaela had spoken healing into his dying body. She had not only cared for him for days, she had healed him and looked like an angel of mercy while doing it. True, she could not speak normally, but she had managed to restore him from the brink of death, with eyes that glowed like a Celestial Spectacle. Her fire was formidable—so strange—but beautiful and *powerful*.

He shook his head. Such considerations were futile. She would never willingly have him. And he did not feel for her as he should. Neither of them deserved to be ensnared like this.

Serenos, their friendly guide, entered the tent. "Are we ready, sir?"

"You will expect us to make pledges we do not mean," Rowan reasoned. "This is not holy. It is a fallacy."

The man clucked at him. "You seem able enough to care for a wife. I saw you fight. And she seems a sweet little woman. You will be content."

"*No!*" Rowan roared. "We will not. I cannot permit this! We will refrain from making the pledges."

The man's face became fury. "Then you will not deliver the recompense for your tribe! We will not release you from this clan until you have been made right." As if reining himself in, he ended quietly, "We cannot, in *conscience*, allow you to travel in sin."

"But... but I give you my word that we have journeyed with utter virtue. And this union would be a lie. Is *that* not a transgression?"

"It is *your* choice whether you make your pledge falsely, whether you keep your vows," Serenos replied somberly. It was clear matrimony was a profound matter to him, even if he was willing to thrust young people into it willy-nilly. With the shaking of his head, he commanded, "Now, come along."

Rowan growled as he concluded he had but to follow. There was no way out in this tent. His only hope was that a way would present itself in due course.

Creator, he thought into the heavens, *spare us a doomed alliance, I beg you.* He had never prayed so before. He had never been in such a position before. Prior to this quest, he had never realized how helpless he could be made to be.

Escorted through the cheering crowds, his pride crumbled away from him. So much for Rowan the *Champion*—a hero who could not even save himself, let alone those with him. If he was fortunate enough to return home, he would be no hero. He would likely be but a husband.

⇢⇢⟩ ⟨⟨⟨⟵

Jaela could not repress the frustrated tear that escaped her eye as she glanced into the reflective glass. She had seen but a fragment of such glass only once before. That one had displayed a filthy, ugly, unloved girl. She had thrust the piece back into the hands of the traveling merchant who tried to sell it to her.

This reflection, however, presented beauty for which she had yearned so long. She had not realized she could look this way, with her typically frizzy hair now prodded into ringlets that bounced down her back. Her skin glistened with cleanliness and the discontented shadows under her eyes had inexplicably cleared. The gown was a pure white weave even tighter than her mother's. Apparently, the skill of weaving had been passed to this tribe at some point in history. It draped over her form with modest majesty, making her appear something like a queen... something like her *mother*. Perhaps not so beautiful as she had always dreamed but not so repulsive as previously presumed.

She had discovered she could look *nice*... and it was to be wasted on an unwanted ceremony with one who detested her speech as well as his ability to comprehend it. He would only be humiliated by her, spending the remainder of his life running from the alliance.

"Come along, ye silent little dear," bade the cheery woman who had cleansed her hands. "He is *waiting.*"

Jaela's stomach contorted painfully. How she wished Rowan waited for her with willingness... with affection or even fondness. But she was the wild thing of her tribe. She would never be loved beyond that of her mother and her one friend. What would she do after this ceremony? What would Rowan do?

They would not be free to wed another for true affection—not that she had ever thought it possible in her case. Well, they would lead independent lives. It was the only option. She would not see him trapped with her. Perhaps he could go to live where none knew of him or their loathed union.

Piloted through applauding crowds, she caught sight of Briar among them. The girl's brows rose high on her head before offering a nod of approval. She, too, noticed Jaela looked better.

Why couldn't this be a different day, another occasion, anything but what it was?

Jaela froze upon sight of Rowan standing in wait down the aisle formed by the celebrating villagers. He was so fetching, but he was not looking her way. He was visibly miserable. At least a dozen men stood behind him, staffs at the ready.

She could not go on. Stealing a tentative step back, she attempted to race through the crowd. But she was thrust back into the path, her delicate veil righted by the women behind her as if they were her bridal attendants.

All she could do was resist looking up again. She could not meet his eyes. After that ruckus, he must have noticed her approach. What must he be thinking?

The situation became all too real as she traversed the steps that led to where he and the tribe leader stood at the ready. She could bear it no longer. She had to look, had to communicate with him that she wanted this no more than he, though he was such a catch.

To her astonishment, his eyes met hers like the dawning of the sun, with brows as high on his forehead as his sister's had been. His gaze revealed mystification, almost as if he was uncertain who she was. She dropped her gaze in perplexity. She had seen herself in the glass. She did not look *that* different, did she? Perhaps merely being clean and properly attired was all it took to bewilder a young man. Then again, perhaps she had misread his expression entirely. It could be he was surprised she had met him at the altar—that he blamed her for not escaping.

But why hadn't *he* done something? He was *Rowan* of Deerskin, son of Bowan the Champion, was he not? If anyone could, it was him. Thrusting the blame back, she reproached him in the glimpse that followed. The glow that she had convinced herself was not there was struck as if by an arrow. He was shocked, humbled, humiliated. And why shouldn't he be when he was about to be wedded to the wild thing?

Something snapped in Jaela. She peered about at those who surrounded. They became daemonkind in her vision. With a roar, she blasted her fire over the tribal leader, turning to shout curses over those surrounding. She leaped from the podium but was caught by numerous hands and shoved back up. Wildly, she searched for what effect she managed only to find the people of Covenants staring up at her as if she were precisely what Deerskin had always deemed her.

The elderly tribe leader cleared his throat, casting a glance of sympathy at Rowan. *Now* they understood the mistake they made in trapping him into an eternal alliance with one who breathed fire and uttered nonsense that she could not even comprehend herself.

Nevertheless, they continued as if nothing had occurred. Rowan's voice repeated the vows that were put to him. He had a dozen guards at his back, after all. When she chanced a glance at him, he was not disgusted by her display. Pity shone in his eyes. An apology. It was as if he was sorry for her own sake.

It was her turn to repeat the pledges. She looked to him with wide eyes. What could she do? If she recited them, it was final.

There was no going back. She had attempted her last resort to no avail. Her gaze flew to Briar, who nodded. She could not make out what the girl thought. Surely, it would be mortifying to be related to someone like Jaela. It would disgrace their family's revered name.

A solid tap to her back revealed she had her own guard now, staffs at the ready. The tribe leader repeated the line he had been urging her to speak. Breathlessly, she did so, her fire curling into Rowan's face. She peered into his eyes with helplessness. He took her hands in his, squeezing them with assurance. He was *with* her. They endured this together. He understood she could do nothing as she understood he could not, else they would not be here. They must persevere in order to complete their critical mission.

Therefore, she swallowed and repeated the remainder. Hand in hand, they were made to turn and face the bizarre audience who cheered riotously. Rowan helped her from the dais as they were ushered back through the path formed by the assemblage. She gripped his hand in fear and trembling at what had just transpired. They were married. She, *Jaela,* had formed a union... with none other than Rowan of Deerskin.

CHAPTER 19

THE THREE TRAVELED IN silence, their faces pasted to the path presented them by the Clan of Covenants. They had been bested and they were in shock. Rowan was, at least. He was a *married man*. Jaela was a married woman. Chatty Briar was the only one who had come through unscathed and even she was reluctant to break the silence.

They had been served a swift wedding meal that none of them had managed an appetite for. Perhaps it was wise they stop for a time, with the sun set so high and the boisterous complaints of Briar's stomach sounding off. But Rowan could not bring himself to speak. He was uncertain of how to *tread*. How did pledged men walk? Was he doing it right? He shook his head at these nonsensical insecurities.

What astounded him most was how much his dread of the ceremony had dissipated at sight of Jaela adorned in her bridal attire. Was he truly so shallow that he minded her less now she proved a stunning partner? She had always been so unkept that he had assumed her looks were born of her deceased father—a

fairly unsightly man. If she had changed of late, he had scarcely thought to notice. Now, he discovered that the beauties he
had glimpsed through her kindnesses and considerations, in her
moments of bravery and power, could be outwardly beheld.

Yet... as he recalled Elaine's beauty, he knew Jaela's was very
different from hers. Elaine's was observable before ever speaking
to her, while Jaela's blazed out from within, something that
might not be thoroughly discerned except by knowing her. He
was mysteriously gratified that he did.

He would be gladder still if he could have realized it under
alternative circumstances. It was overwhelming to face now that
she was his *wife*. He did not know what to make of a wife. He
wasn't prepared for one, certainly wasn't worthy of her.

It occurred to him that the entire incident had been his fault.
He was the one who had led them into the Forbidden Pass. He
had been ready for the kind of peril he was trained to face—not
a wedding. How many had been entangled before the clans had
marked the path as forbidden? If he had possessed the good
sense to give up or find another way, Jaela would not have been
placed in this situation. Yet, he could not regret the decision
entirely. Though they were forever tied, there still lay a chance
for their tribe.

Even so... it was difficult to look upon Jaela's misery. He
recalled how fiercely she had fought to escape the marriage.
Unconsciously, he had taken it for granted that she would be
less repulsed by the situation due to who he was. Every young
lady he came in contact with, save Elaine, had been obviously

interested. But Jaela did not share their sentiment. She felt as trapped as he did.

And yet... was it his imagination or did he feel less ensnared than he had expected at the outset? Each time he managed a sidelong glimpse at her, he was puzzled by his lack of dismay. He could not claim he was swooning with adoration. But he really didn't mind her. In truth, he esteemed her. She was nothing like his people thought. He had already determined in his heart to make that right for her own sake. Was appreciation enough to make for a pleasant alliance?

"I *cannot* go on without something in my stomach," Briar finally announced.

Rowan nodded. "We will need our strength if we are to find the entrance to the Nethers before nightfall."

Without word or glance, Jaela seated herself against a nearby tree. She folded her arms together, not looking up. Rowan exchanged looks with his sister. To his relief, she took the initiative of taking Jaela's pack from him and carrying it to her. The two proceeded to sit where Jaela had settled. Rowan blinked back disorientation once again to find her sitting like a lily of the valley in the noon light. She really was not unsightly. Even if she were, he felt certain her internal loveliness would alter her outwardly. Maybe it was even now and he was only fooling himself. But he did not seem to care. His real trouble was that he had no idea how to act around her anymore. Where was his typical bravado?

"You must eat, Jaela," Briar urged, passing her a satchel of spiced seeds.

Rowan shook his head. "She does not care for those." He reached into his pack to pass the remaining cake his mother had sent. One needed to be tempted with something truly tasty in situations such as these and she required strength. He looked up in time to catch her stunned expression before she accepted it.

They continued in silence. Rowan thought he would go mad if this persisted the remainder of their expedition. He could not remain on tenterhooks for so long. He wasn't accustomed to it. It made him queasy.

"*So...* I have a sister now," Briar spoke of a sudden. "Always wanted one, you know."

Jaela's eyed flooded with tears unshed as they flew to Briar's face.

Briar squeezed Jaela's hand in a comradely way. "I am glad I discovered how much I liked you in time," she added to her prior sentiment. "And Rowan's a bit of a wild thing himself, so far as all that goes."

To Rowan's surprise, Jaela's tears dropped from her eyes to the accompaniment of relieved chortling. Before long, he added his own.

"I mean, the fellow's a *mess*," Briar added matter-of-factly. "You should see his quarters back home. The floor is *plastered* with weapons, spent tunics and the like. One might think there had been a massacre if they had not grown up with his ways."

Rowan blushed under the divulgences, wishing his sister would keep quiet while silently thanking her for relieving the moment. He was even more grateful when Jaela covered her mouth due to persistent laughter, to which even Briar finally broke down.

"I had better warn you about his *singing*," Briar continued with sudden gravity. "It is like no birdsong you ever awoke to. I tell you, I once bolted up in a state of fright, thinking he or father were in some kind of peril."

"Ho-*ho!*" Rowan broke in. "You are no better yourself, little duckie."

"Assuredly," the sister confessed, "but at least I know it. You seem to entertain notions of inevitable renown, the way you go on." She looked to Jaela with the shake of her head. "He sounds like a dying toad."

By this point, Jaela was bent with laughter. Rowan could not find it all so funny himself, but he supposed the mere relief of jesting after what had transpired was enough to send her to riots. This vision of her smiling both relieved and burdened him. He wanted to keep her smiling. He didn't ever want her to stop smiling—at least not on his account. If Briar had to lay him out in utter flaw before her, it was worth it if Jaela would only laugh instead of cry.

***

Jaela was grateful when Rowan suggested they take to the woods on either side of the path in order to change from their fine attire. It had been difficult walking in such heavy garments. She soon found herself holding her gown, attempting to decide what was to be done with it. Part of her wished to fling it into the wilderness in good riddance. It had come from *them*. She could not bear the thought of the people who had done this to her. At the same time... it was her matrimonial garment. Was it callous to get rid of it?

But what was callous in a marriage like theirs? Would she ever be able to find it within herself to look back at the memory with anything like cheer? Would she ever desire to pull out her white garment in order to relive it? Of course not. She tossed it into the bushes.

Marching several steps from the spot, she inevitably froze. It was after some moments' contemplation that she went back to retrieve it, stuffing it into the bottom of her pack in hopes she would not have to face it again until she was back home and her mother could tell her what to do about it.

That was, if they made it home. The Clan of Covenants had not seemed so sure.

"You will be grateful we guided you into virtue when you stand before your Creator," Serenos had voiced. With a look of exasperating sorrow, he added, "Which may not be long before you now. I wish you a celestial journey, fortunate couple and sister. May you walk in righteousness for the remainder of your existence."

That in mind, Jaela returned to the path with, "They promised this trail led to a secondary passage into the Nethers... What do we do if they have told a falsehood?"

She had not realized the ease with which she spoke until Rowan blinked back at her with scarcely concealed surprise. But he replied readily enough.

"I do not believe they would lie. It would go against their code of righteousness."

She nodded, turning to Briar, who watched them in confusion. It was a moment before Jaela recalled that the girl could not understand a thing she spoke.

"Well, this is just *great,*" Briar declared, "now *I* am the odd man out. Can someone inform me of what we are deliberating, here?"

Jaela was surprised to find herself chuckling again. If Briar thought this was bad, she ought to try nearly a decade without friendship.

"We have just decided this path must be what it was promised to be," Rowan explained. "I do not think they would lie."

Jaela nodded. "Let us hurry on." She was ready to put the recent episode behind her for a time. "I am—"

A rumbling underfoot caused their forms to tremble. Trees danced and pebbles bounced under the reverberations. Their eyes were drawn to an afternoon sky overshadowed with inexplicable darkness. Soon to follow were lightning strikes that flooded the atmosphere with immersive thunder, though no precipitation followed.

It was some time they stood as if waiting for a conclusion. But Jaela realized they must go on. She was certain these happenings had something to do with what HS had alluded to. *Something* was happening or soon would. The son of the Great One dwelled upon another planet in another *universe...* What could have possibly befallen to send echoes even onto the planes of Kaern?

"This portends danger," Briar called over the thunder. "We should find shelter!"

Jaela shook her head. "We must hasten."

Rowan pursed his lips together in contemplation as the quaking underfoot took him off balance. "Do you have reason for such urgency, Jaela?"

She nodded before continuing their trek.

Next thing she knew, he was beside her. "Well?"

She nearly released another laugh, so unaccustomed was she to communicating her purposes. "You recall the being who made me—made us—what we are?" She watched his face for how he would respond to her use of "us."

Not seeming to notice, he nodded with interest.

"That was the spirit-essence of the Creator, the Great One," she explained. "He... befriended me."

"I am aware," he answered with a nod. "Though, I had not *begun* to guess who he was."

"He tells me something unusual is taking place over the course of this recompense. I do not thoroughly understand it. I just know I do not wish to miss whatever it may be."

"I do not believe we are missing out," he answered, gesturing to the atmosphere as they marched upon a quaking Kaern that was only just beginning to calm.

With a nod, she turned her gaze away. This back-and-forth exchange was markedly relieving, even if it was with a compulsory spouse. Instantly, she realized she could not think of him as such. They must focus on the task at hand, something she sensed they were drawing very near. She questioned if their initial undertaking would be accomplished or if another would overshadow it—her recompense paid in full, forever.

Rowan explained Jaela's haste to Briar. It was clear the girl was startled by his claim that Jaela knew the Creator... face to face. But in the end, she seemed to look on her with awe. For the first time in Jaela's life, she comprehended how rare and impossible her friendship with HS was. Though she loved him, he had become so true and close a friend that she had taken him for granted. And he had let her. What kind of God was this? And what would he require of her when the time came for which he had called her out?

Though Rowan did not reveal it outwardly, he was whiplashed by Jaela's confession. He had known she kept clandestine communication with the being who had altered her. He had *not* gathered it was the Creator of the universe. And *his wife* knew him personally? He could not help feeling daunted by the notion.

As they continued under an overcast sky, he found himself distracted by the gratification of walking beside her. How could a single journey alter so much so swiftly? At the onset, anyone would have said she was lucky to be involved with him. All of the sudden, he felt himself the fortunate party. And it was a novel sentiment. Despite his feelings of unworthiness through the years, he had maintained a deal of self-importance. By this point, that was debris in the wind.

These revelations were eventually dominated by the unnatural display around them. What could possibly be causing it? Jaela had mysteriously alluded to some unusual event. He prayed it would not hinder their delivery of the recompense. Though he could no longer harbor hopes of returning home a hero, he wanted to do what was right.

An enormous mountain soon materialized ahead. It was either the end of their path or the continuance of it. Squinting to gather more detail revealed a massive fissure. Could it be the entrance to the Nethers? He no longer felt himself prepared for what lay ahead, which was unnerving. Casting a sidelong glance at Briar, he wondered if she felt the same.

"You think Farrow and Elaine will be waiting somewhere in there?" she asked. "You know, since I stole the recompense for their tribe..."

Rowan considered this. "Either that or they have given up."

Briar raised a brow. "Good thing *I* have it then, eh?"

Nay, his sister had not changed a bit. He was glad of it. She was a superior version of who he had thought himself to be, for she at least possessed the humility derived from not attaining their parents' total approval. Contrary to his prior suppositions, he was astounded to find humility was so precious. Arrogance had led him to what had appeared to be his downfall twice over. And was not Jaela's unpretentiousness what proved to make her even more extraordinary? After all, she *performed miracles* without ever batting an eye.

Question was, who would *he* prove to be henceforth?

The three stopped as the cave mouth loomed overhead. Rowan consulted the map. It appeared as if their path led into the same mountain they were meant to have entered from the other side. If they had taken that path, it was almost certain they would have been too late. Yet, this course had cost two of them their liberty. He really hoped it was worth it.

With a jolting gasp, Jaela dropped to the ground. Rowan plunged to his knees beside her, flooded with trepidation. Had she been shot by an arrow? There did not seem to be one any-where.

"What *is* it?" he questioned.

It seemed an age before she blinked up at him with tears in her eyes. "I *saw* him—the son of the Great One. He is *dying...*" Her body convulsed with a sob.

Rowan raised his brows. Was this a vision she referred to? Some within the tribes were known to experience them. He simply had not realized she was one of them. Was it a regular occurrence? But even more baffling was what she claimed.

"Since when does the Creator have a son, Jaela?" he questioned.

"He hangs from wood by the grasp of *spikes,*" she sobbed out, thrusting her face into her hands as her body wrenched with sorrow.

Rowan looked to his sister, lost for what to think or do. Few experienced such intense visionary experiences. Briar's face conveyed she was as adrift as he. Yet, she knelt at the other side of the sobbing girl as if to support her with her mere presence. Perhaps that was all he could offer as well.

Jaela's eyes pierced him. "You do not understand. He is... *everything*. He is God and... he is *dying.*" Her face was smothered by her hands again. The underground rumblings re-commenced as she murmured, *"Father... forgive them, for they know not what they do."*

Lightning and thunder initiated around them. As chills besieged Rowan's body, he hastily scooped Jaela up off the ground. He and Briar raced into the cavernous mouth. Gentling resting Jaela back upon the ground, he pulled her hands from her face.

"Jaela, forgive *who?*" his voice echoed throughout the cavern. "What is happening?"

"They are killing him," she choked out. "And he is *letting* them." Her large eyes fixed on him like a lifeline.

All he could manage was to blink back with uncertainty, no idea of what to make of her mutterings. He might have considered that she had lost her senses due to the strain of their forced union if this paroxysm of the world itself had not accompanied her declarations.

"Look..." he finally began, "I know it may be difficult, but you said yourself we must hasten. There is no telling how far we have yet to travel. The sun can no longer denote the time of day or night."

Jaela nodded like a child bidden to quit her tantrum. Rowan helped brush the tears from her cheeks before helping her to her feet. Briar's part was to fix up a torch. She appeared ready to light it when Jaela blew it into flame and took it in hand. With fortitude that stunned the siblings, she started onward.

Jaela's heart throbbed as they traversed the cavern. She was torn between eagerness and terror of reaching their destination. But she felt certain that whatever HS wished her to witness would transpire within the Nethers. Therefore, she was determined. Even so, she worried that the Anointed One had been bested.

Aside from her dream that morning, Jaela had never received a vision before. This one had entered her mind's eye like a waking dream. She presumed it was presented by HS, which made it all too true. Had the Anointed One succeeded in accomplishing his objective before being nailed to the wooden torture device? She shuddered at the awful recollection of his brutalized body. It made her march all the swifter.

A tunnel emerged at the back of the cavern. Not knowing what else to do, they took this course. It wasn't until they reached the end that they feared they had been led astray. With something like queasiness, they peered down into a dark abyss. To the right, stood a signpost.

"A leap of faith," Briar read, "into Death's realm. Enter at your peril." After some moments, she added, "Are we... supposed to jump or something?"

The three gazed further in, but all that met them was blackness.

"It is suicide," Briar finally muttered, stepping away.

Jaela and Rowan followed suit.

"Could this have been a trick?" Jaela asked of Rowan.

He stole a long breath. Before she knew it, he was rolling up his sleeves. "There is only one way to find out."

She grasped his arm. "You are not *seriously* jumping, Rowan of Deerskin?"

"Worried?" he asked with a wink.

She released her grip, stepping back as she blinked away consternation. "No, I... think it foolhardy."

"Well, in that case," he answered easily, pulling open his pack. "We shall use this." He withdrew a rope.

Jaela huffed despite the smirk that crept onto her face. "Well, you are too heavy for us."

"Briar is not," he replied. "I can manage her weight on my own."

Briar raised a brow. "Very well. But I am chugging some kempur first."

Jaela was surprised by Briar's need. Kempur was a beverage that was meant to boost one's vitality, concentration and boldness. She had never envisioned Briar as the sort who necessitated aid in those areas. Nevertheless, the girl poured the powder into her waterskin and guzzled as if her life depended on it. This did nothing to soothe Jaela's nerves.

"She does not relish heights," Rowan explained, "or drops."

Jaela raised her brows. She had never guessed when they were encamped upon the mountaintop. "Perhaps I should do it," she offered tremulously.

Briar shook her head as if she grasped Jaela's utterance. "I do not chicken out of *anything,* Jaela of Deerskin."

"Besides," Rowan went on, "we have done this a hundred times, her and I. We were a couple of young adventurers growing up."

Jaela could not help but smile as she pictured the two getting themselves into scrapes that their parents must have loathed. Yet, they had raised courageous children whom she admired.

With the rope tied snuggly about Briar, she planted her feet on the edge of the cliff, her back facing the abyss below her. "So help me, Rowan, if you drop me, I will *haunt* you."

"Noted," he answered with a grin.

Jaela's gaze went from one to the other. They *enjoyed* this—the danger. They were made for it. She shook her head at them. When it came to situations such as this, they were the best company she could have asked for.

"So far, so good," Briar reported as she ambled down the rock-wall. "A little wet, perhaps... slippery," she added with a squeal as the skidding of her feet echoed up at them.

Rowan's previous candor was replaced by resolute attentiveness. "You all right?" he called.

"Sure thing," Briar answered as the sound of her steps continued.

It felt an age they breathed anxiety before Briar next narrated, "There is something below. It is... light."

Rowan and Jaela exchanged glances.

"What is light?" he probed.

"It is too *bright*—"

Her scream split the atmosphere as the rope was wrenched from Rowan's hands.

"Briar!" he bellowed into the darkness.

The pair at the top fell to the edge as if they might glimpse something of Briar.

No response followed.

"I am sorry," Rowan murmured to Jaela with a significant glance.

Before Jaela could stop him, he was gone. She fell back with a shriek. What had he just done? Ended his life because he had failed Briar? She recalled how the rope had fled his hands. It was unnatural, as if Briar had been swept away in a breath. Perhaps Rowan believed there was something beyond the light, something that may *not* lead to death? More likely, he had not cared. If there was a chance he could aid his sister, he would take it. His recklessness proved his devotion. But now Jaela sat alone. And what was she to do? Would he manage somehow to return with his sister? Was she to wait on those she may never see again?

Her body trembled as she breathed into the dim light of the torch. Her own fire flooded the expanse due to her stilted gasps. Why had he done it? Why had he not told her what he intended, or what she was to do? She glanced at the packs. Perhaps she was now left to find another way to deliver their recompenses. But *how?*

If they were truly gone... how was she meant to go on? Somehow, they had become friends, at least on her end. She cared for them. Briar was dear as a sister—*was,* unbelievably, a sister now. Rowan was... well, he was the one she had dragged through a forest for days on end. She had saved his life and for what? To lose him like *this?* Her heart physically stung with sorrow she could not have foreseen. She bit her hand in an effort to stifle it, but her spirit surged with emotions she had not desired to acknowledge. Feelings, however, *would* grow and fester of their own accord and now she was—

A rock shot up from the abyss, plummeting downward again. She raced to the edge. Some moments later, the stone returned again, this time flying so fast it hit the ceiling and bounced upon the floor not far from where she knelt. Sailing upon it, she cradled it in her hands. The corresponding ring that Rowan had been given for their avowals was fixed tightly to it with a leather cord. Her eyes returned to the abyss.

Could it truly be they were alive, that this was a sign of it... perhaps even an invitation to join them? Her gaze flew to the signpost. "A leap of faith." Maybe it wasn't a trick. It must not be, else how could she be holding his matrimonial ring?

Tossing the rock into Rowan's pack, she cast it over the edge. Next went Briar's. Finally, her own. Her heart raced with what she was doing. But now the supplies were gone, there was no going back.

Problem was... thrusting herself into the unknown as Rowan had done proved completely beyond her nature. Tears pricked her eyes as she clutched her arms, glaring down into the dark. She dropped to her rear, biting her lower lip in frustration.

"HS?" she called into the atmosphere. "You promised you were always with me, that you would care for me. Well, I *believe* you... and I need your help now. Help me do this or stop me, if you will."

The words had scarcely left her tongue when she was encompassed by a swirling breeze that tossed her hair and clothes. It was like a breath from the very mouth of her friend. He truly was here. And he was not stopping her. She stood to her feet, hands clenched into fists. Taking a breath as if prepared to leap into water, she stepped into nothing.

Her body plummeted faster than she had anticipated. Ruthlessly, it snuffed the breath from her. She knew she must soon perish and prayed only that HS would catch her on the other side—with or without a recompense.

As suddenly as it appeared in her vision, she was absorbed into a flash of light. She closed her eyes to its blinding radiance as her body suddenly floated as if weightless. In the next moment, she was tumbling painfully down a rocky slope before being scooped up by a pair of arms. Opening her eyes with uncertainty, she found Rowan smiling over her.

"Celestial day, Jaela of Deerskin. Welcome to the Nethers."

CHAPTER 20

JAELA PEERED INTO THE hazy darkness. Fire burned like torches along the rocky ridges of towering ramparts. A perpetual wind pelted her with scorching air that resounded with an incessant roar, like that of a waterfall in the distance. What sent her flying back was the grotesque daemon that stood beyond Rowan and Briar.

"It is all right," Rowan assured, stumbling after her. "At least... as all right as can be expected." Pulling her to her feet, he turned to the daemon. "This is Tremulous, our, er, guide to the Cauldron of Recompense."

Jaela blinked at the creature who leered at her with an odious grin. The smile dropped as he thrust a finger in her face. "There'll be none of your funny business down here, *firetongue*," he warned. "Else you won't be present for the delivery of your recompense."

She blinked back, having nearly forgotten what she had done to the previous sprites who had harmed them. But hadn't those been attempting to stop them from doing precisely what Tremulous claimed he would lead them to?

"We cannot trust him," she spoke openly.

"Of course you can't," the daemon sniveled. "But try making your own way and see where it gets you in these parts. You're in daemon realms now, girly." He turned his back on them to start onward.

Jaela grasped Rowan's arm. "I do not trust him."

"I do not trust him either, but..."

"We do not know what else to do," Briar finished.

Jaela's eyes shot to Rowan. "Briar can see him?"

"Seems so," he answered with a shrug. "Perhaps because we're on their turf now?"

Jaela blew out a long breath, her fire illuminating the expanse more fiercely than was customary.

"Breathe again," Rowan urged.

"Why?" she inquired.

He thrust his hand into her fire. With bewilderment, he explained, "It is cool."

"Sure, it is cool," Briar put in, "compared to the flames of the *Nethers*." She swept a line of sweat from her brow. "Let us get *on*."

Rowan exchanged a glance with Jaela before he began, "Look, I understand your fire does not seem to harm us humans, but... I have seen what you can do to their kind. If at any moment you have need and get the chance, do not hesitate to use it in order to escape—even if it means leaving us behind. We both know they want you for some other purpose... And although I believe they may actually fear you, I do not know what they will do once we have completed our task."

Jaela's eyes narrowed as she brushed past him. "I do not plan on leaving anyone behind should the possibility arise," she called back. Owing to his leap into an abyss, she had already experienced what it would feel like to be without them. "But thanks again for the vote of confidence."

He raced to her side. "That is *not* what I meant. I just worry that you are in more danger than us, being what you are."

"Right—a *wild thing*. I understand. Let us just catch up, shall we?"

"*No,*" he nearly shouted with the wrenching of her arm. "You are *not* a wild thing."

"What am I then?"

"You are... *impossible.*"

She blinked back at him, uncertain of his connotation. In the end, she determined he was frustrated with her. The light in his eyes intimated other things. Or was it a reflection of the flickering flames above? But his opinion was of little consequence at the moment. There were games afoot and they must determine to survive them, as numerous others had managed in all the years before. She moved on without comment.

The Nethers proved to run like a maze of coiling tunnels. Tremulous had not spoken falsely when he had intimated they could not find their own way. More likely, they would have been lost for days, if not forever.

What struck Jaela was the desolation of the place. She had always believed the Nethers was the dark one's kingdom. But with cells and chains appearing every other turn, it appeared more like an expansive dungeon. Question was, why were there no prisoners as yet? And where were the, er, dead housed?

She stopped short as they took the right shoulder of a fork in the path. The three looked to one another with widened eyes. What had sounded akin to the roar of falling water in the distance now echoed frantically through the passage.

"Is that...?" Briar whispered hoarsely.

None would speak what they knew it to be. It was too dreadful a reality to put into words. The raucously maddening resonance was a vast chorus of *anguish*. Somewhere at the core of this realm lay the stuff of darkest legend. This was the hereafter of the dead.

"Not far now," Tremulous informed in a low voice.

Jaela and the others leaped in place before following his retreating frame. His nonchalance was enough to put Jaela even further on edge. Was he truly guiding them to this "Cauldron of Recompense?" Or would he lead them on and on until they collapsed from mere exhaustion?

The heat was too dizzying to allow for much meditation. The three dripped with sweat. Breathing was laborious. Their water supply was gone. The only one truly holding her own was Briar, who had enjoyed a generous supply of kempur before dropping into this accursed place. What Jaela wouldn't do for a drought of it.

Without warning, Tremulous paused. His gaze traveled to the lofty ceiling overheard. It was a moment before Jaela could determine why. It was soon apparent that the reverberations occurring in her world were reaching this one as well. As the quakes commenced, her vision was seized once again.

"It... is... finished..." she cried involuntarily.

As she fell to her knees, the Nethers quailed beyond anything they had experienced. She sensed the others fall beside her as she witnessed the Anointed One's chin drop to his chest. He was *gone*. Dead. No more. The only son of the Great One was finished. It was awful, unfeasible, criminal.

The quaking did not subside with his death. It intensified. The very walls around them trembled and swayed as if they would cave in. There was no continuing on. There was only the prayer for survival.

At long last, the terrain ceased its moaning. Somewhere in the distance, they perceived screeches of sheer glee, along with music and the stamping of feet. Now that Jaela's vision was clear, she searched for Tremulous, but he was long gone. They were on their own. She deduced he had fled to join his brethren in their revelry. But if the Anointed One's death was their victory, these realms of darkness were his enemy. If they were rivals, the recompense, as she knew it, was a sham... was it not?

Rowan's hand went to her back. "He is... dead?"

Tears dripped from her jawline as she nodded.

His face expressed a series of reactions before he mutely helped her and Briar to their feet.

"I suppose we find our own way now?" Briar asked shakily. It seemed the display had gotten to her. It had affected Jaela, too. She shivered over the loss of one she had never even known. And she was terrified. If daemonkind could best the Great One, what couldn't they do to her and those she loved?

"Are you all right to walk?" Rowan questioned with concern.

Almost mirthfully, she wondered what he would do if she wasn't. "Y-yes," she hiccupped.

He nodded before continuing with her arm in his grasp. She could not claim she was not grateful. Her vision was blurred with tears for the one who sent daemons to flight, who healed the sick and even raised the dead. He was the only one she had ever seen who was even close to being like herself... But he had been *so much more*. He was *God*... and he was gone. Where did that leave them? Where did it leave the recompense? What had happened to HS's promises?

⇝⇜

Rowan paused as he read the signpost above the next cave mouth: *Cauldron of Recompense*. Stepping through with Briar beside him and Jaela in tow, it whiplashed him how different everything was now he was finally here. He had expected to go marching in like a true champion. Jaela was to have been in tow merely because she was helpless and afraid. Briar wasn't to have been present at all, nor presenting her own share of recompense.

Instead, *he* was afraid. Jaela was grief-stricken due to supernatural visions concerning a son of the Creator, though he could

not fathom what it had to do with anything. Briar, usually un-
daunted, quivered beside him. Even so, her march was as stolid
as ever, as if flinging her fear back into the face of the Nethers.

The room was more ornately adorned than anything they had
seen as yet. The walls were of the same reddish rock and the
breadth was illuminated by the perimeter of flame along the
upper crests. But it was the golden, bejeweled lampstands on
either side of each step of a broad case of stairs that denoted this
was a favored ritual. The opulent carpet that ran from where
they stood to the upper landing ended beneath a large cauldron
from which a trail of smoke curled indifferently. A curious ray
of red light shone from overhead to illuminate it. Undoubtedly,
this was their destination—the very location for which they had
set out nearly a fortnight prior.

Rowan turned to Briar as if in question of what to do next.
Did they simply march up the stairs and drop the gems in?

Briar shrugged. "Let us—" Her words were dashed by a brute
force that tackled her to the ground.

"How *dare* you steal the recompense of Blooms?!" Farrow
roared into her face.

Elaine rushed in to pull Farrow off by the strap of his pack.
"You utter *crackpot!*" she barked. "She is *here*. That is all that
matters!"

Rowan strode into the melee, plucking Farrow from his sister
and thrusting him against the nearest wall. "That will be enough
of that!" he informed severely.

"Well," Elaine huffed, blowing a lose lock from her face, "that about settles it." She offered her hand to him. "Good to finally see you conscious, Ro."

Rowan was surprised by her apparent gratification of meeting him again. His kneejerk reaction was to be pleased to see her until it hit him that he was no longer free to feel such satisfaction concerning another girl. Almost before he had processed this, he watched her gaze find his finger. Though he had tossed his marital ring to Jaela as a sign to leap into the abyss, something had compelled him to restore it to his finger.

Elaine's brows rose in confusion. "What happened with *you* folks?"

His gaze sought Jaela, who glared boldly up at the cauldron as if she had not noticed the commotion. Curiously, a swell of pride stirred within him. Perhaps it was merely vanity, but he was not unhappy to be free of Elaine due to her.

"We took a shortcut," he answered with a smirk, gesturing to where Jaela stood.

Elaine's eyes flew to Jaela's finger. "Well..." she answered in a near choke. *"Some* shortcut.... I congratulate you both."

"Hand over the recompense!" Farrow roared at Briar as he nursed his bruised arm.

Briar stood with arms crossed, sneering back. "And why do you not just *take* it, Farrow? You fear my brother, eh?"

"This has nothing to do with your brother!" he retorted. "This is about the delivery and you are in no way worthy of representing Blooms. This is up to me and Elaine."

Briar rolled her eyes. "Neither you nor Elaine are the ones in possession of it, are you now?" She turned her back to him, starting up the stairs. Farrow grappled for her pack-strap.

"I said that was enough," Rowan reminded with a growl.

Farrow fell back. "This is not *just* and you know it, Rowan of Deerskin," he fairly howled. "She *stole* our recompense! And what if she had not made it in time? Our tribe would have been obliterated because of *her.*"

"Like I said before," Elaine began, "she is here. Let us... do it together." Her eyes queried Briar.

Briar shook her head. "If you help, they will write me out of the story. I have wanted this glory for as long as I can remember."

Elaine searched her for some moments, likely considering what she was willing to give up. In the end, she nodded. "Do it," she demanded of Farrow, "the two of you. Just... make certain the tribe knows I was here when it was accomplished."

Farrow shook his head. "It is not right."

"It is," Elaine admitted with a sigh. "She was chosen. I was not. Go on now, the four of you."

"Patience, champions," an elegant voice echoed through the chamber.

Rowan twirled to find they were no longer alone. A majestic figure with trailing gold robes climbed the stairs on the opposite end of the cauldron's landing. Though he slightly resembled the daemons they had previously encountered, there was something more humanoid in his makeup. He appeared more like a towering, handsome prince. Rowan was struck by his cockiness, the arrogance that oozed from every twitch of his brow. Absently, he wondered if this was how he had come across before this expedition. He shivered to think it.

"I do not typically perform this ceremony myself," began the imperious daemon as he reached the top, "but I elected to step from the celebration of my greatest victory when I learned the only remaining firetongue in the realms had invaded my domain."

As Rowan's stomach turned, his eyes flashed to Jaela, who paled considerably concerning those words.

"Humbly..." Rowan began with the clearing of his throat, "I would not call it an invasion. She was specifically selected to deliver the recompense for the Tribe of Deerskin."

The daemon's brow rose as his eyes exchanged Jaela for Rowan. "If it isn't the son of Bowan, one of the finest champions among my little tribes. Like father, like son, I hope." His gaze swept the small assemblage. "You have a choice to make, my champions."

Abruptly, new voices echoed into the room as two more sets of young people entered. They stopped short when their eyes fell upon the company, ending with the mysterious daemon on the platform.

"*Yes*, yes, welcome!" he called. "Come in, come in! I perceive there are a few others to follow. The more the merrier! I haven't done anything like this in an *eon.*"

The new arrivals shuffled in among the group, looking about in mystification. Rowan felt just as confused. He had not realized the delivery of the recompense would be so formal. By the way many had made it sound, he had expected to fight his way through. Had Jaela's presence altered things? He swallowed back his apprehension, kicking himself for not having left her behind in that cavern in the mountain. He feared they had delivered more than a few rubies to this lover of iniquity.

When three more groups arrived, the supercilious sprite surveyed them for some moments. "As I said before..." he began at last, "you have a decision to make, champions of the tribes. I urge you to make it well."

Considering each member of the crowd in turn, his painted lips curled into a grin at sight of Jaela. "Every annum, two fortunate heroes from each tribe deliver the recompense of salvation from the justification of your iniquities. That is all very well and good, to be sure... But this grave responsibility comes with a tiny little secret which *you,* in your turn, are forbidden from ever sharing beyond the Nethers. Indeed," he added with a laugh, "none ever desire to do so."

Clasping his hands behind his back, he turned to pace first one way and then the other. He stopped to face them again. "Who among you is willing to follow me?"

Silence reigned until Farrow braved the question on the tip of every tongue, "Who *are* you?"

"Wh-who... am... *I?*"

His face contorted into a grotesque scowl as he folded his arms across his chest. When he flung them out again, a torrent of light pierced the atmosphere, transforming his attire into snowy garments that shimmered under the glow of his own form. Upon his head appeared a golden crown with gems that sparkled like fire. "I am... that I *am!*" he boomed. "I am light!"

The whole room radiated with his form.

"I am music!"

The fairest sound Rowan had ever heard played through the atmosphere.

"I am God!"

The atmosphere thundered.

"I am... *Luciferas!*"

The final utterance brought stillness, silence.

Quivering with awe, Rowan was struck by the shaking of Jaela's head. Her eyes brooded with flame. To his further amazement, an affronted Luciferas perceived her motion.

His eyes sparked into flame as he bellowed, "What have *you* got to say for yourself, *firetongue?!*"

To Rowan's utter shock and dismay, she ungraciously professed, "Your light is *borrowed*."

Rowan nearly stepped before her in an effort to stop her, to shield her from impending danger, but she persisted before he had the chance.

"It is the glory absorbed from standing in the presence of one who is not constrained by invention. Rather, he is the author of it. You, on the other hand, cannot even claim the name of Lucifer anymore. You are egotism. You are fallacy. You are created, *dark one*. You are no god."

It wasn't until Briar's eyes sought him that Rowan realized none in the room but him fathomed a word of what she spoke. He wasn't even certain Jaela realized what she was spouting. It certainly didn't sound like her, nor did she entirely look like herself in the conviction she wore like a queen's robe. He admired her audaciousness, from wherever it was derived. But trepidation concerning her safety was at the forefront.

He had not realized just who they were dealing with until she had named this creature. His only hope was that the dark one had not perceived her language either. The dark one's expression had not altered during her speech, nor had his gaze wandered from hers. Slowly, he sauntered down the stairs, taking each step in stride, until he was looming before her.

Drawing near her face, he hissed, "You'll come to understand I am god enough before I am through with you, *mutt.*"

Rowan could bear it no longer. He stepped between them, standing as tall and sturdy as he could muster.

With an amused twinkle, the dark one searched him up and down before precipitously turning on his heel. As if nothing of import had occurred, he paced before his audience, the rays of his pirated light making it difficult to witness his movements.

"Are you ready, children, to deliver the recompense for your tribes?" he questioned in a low tone. "Line up! Chip-chop!"

Some moments' hesitation followed before the champions took to establishing a line by pairs. All that each champion had left to do was drop a single gemstone into the cauldron. Then, it would be finished. Rowan, for one, could not wait to complete the mission, to get Jaela out of the Nethers. He would not feel safe until that was done.

Returning to the upper landing, the dark one spun to face them. "You may begin your deliveries..." he said with a nod, "on one condition. Do not begin to think me unjust when I state this, for *all* those who came before you every annum from the founding of the recompense were rendered the same choice. If your clan remains in existence... it is thanks to the arrangement made between your former champions and myself...

"Follow me!" he roared of a sudden. "Pay allegiance to me and I will make you champions among champions! As my children, you earn the ability to salvage your tribes *and* vacate my domain unscathed. Only remember this: Your soul is mine. Your will is mine. *You* are mine... *Are we agreed?*"

CHAPTER 21

MURMURS RESOUNDED FROM THOSE assembled. Jaela turned to Rowan with question in her eyes. What were they to do? She had witnessed the death of the Creator's son herself. She had understood he was their hope. That hope had died with him.

Before she had time to thoroughly process the dark one's revelations, a pair of champions stepped forward. The young man bellowed pompously, "We are willing to do whatever it takes for the salvation of the Warrior Tribe!"

"Approach, my children," the dark one beckoned, "and release your rubies over the cauldron. The act will seal the contract!"

The champions of the Warrior Tribe started valiantly up the stairs. Jaela wished they would only take a moment to consider. This was the *dark* one. But her speech would not reach them.

"Tell them!" she pleaded with Rowan, grasping his tunic. "Tell them who he is!"

He blinked down at her for some moments, clearly considering whether he was as looney as she was. His eyes flew to the two at the top.

"*Wait!*" Rowan commanded.

Like obedient cadets, the champions turned to face him.

"This is the *dark one*, the legend of our nightmares," he exclaimed. "We must *think!*"

The young male of the Warrior Tribe appraised the illuminated form of the dark one. After some moments, he called to Rowan, "*Nice* try, but it is too late." With the releasing of his gem, he shouted, "It is finished!" Fresh smoke mushroomed from the cauldron, choking the two who stood beside it.

The lad turned to the female champion. "Do it, Phera. Do it now!"

The girl scrutinized her comrade, then Rowan and finally the dark one. Her eyes seemed to favor the luminous glory of the last. With a nod, she dropped her ruby into the cauldron, bourgeoning a suffocating cloud.

"Well done, my children," the dark one cooed, gesturing for them to descend the opposite stairwell. "Right this way. Tremulous is waiting to show you and the remainder of your brothers and sisters back home where you may help to establish my domain. You have become cogs of my magnificent beast. He will disclose *all* the details along the way."

Without warning, Farrow stepped forward. "We are ready!" he shouted with a sidelong summon to Briar.

Briar's eyes flew to her brother's.

"*No!*" Jaela whispered with emotion. "Do not do this. Something is wrong. It is *all* wrong."

Indeed, she was certain it was erroneous. It could not truly be that the salvation of the tribes had been bought and paid for by the souls of their champions. That was not salvation. It was death warmed over. No wonder HS had spoken so resentfully of the recompense. It was a revolting affair. But what could they do? Through the years, they had heard tales of the devastation wrought upon villages whose champions failed their quests. The inhabitants of such places ceased to exist except in memory.

Taking a long breath, Briar nodded to Rowan. "It is what the champions before us have done. I... *must* do this." Her voice cracked. It was clear her show of confidence was just that. "Blooms is counting on me."

Rowan gripped her wrist. "Are you sure?" he questioned intensely.

Her breath came in a small hiccup. Jaela had never seen her like this, so brave yet so terrified. "This is the moment I have... been waiting for." She turned from her brother to walk beside Farrow as they ascended.

Jaela's mind raced with the heating of her blood. An impulse was coming on. Whatever it was, she gave herself to it. Something had to be done. Someone had to stop Briar from throwing her soul away. But it was taking too long to come to culmination. Briar had nearly reached the cauldron. There simply *had* to be another way. The son of the Great One had perished... and what for? Was that the end of it? Had his mission been vanquished prematurely, though he was the son of the Creator of all existence? It could not be... She searched her memory for HS's words. Suddenly, his voice was in her mind. His words were the zenith.

"He has paid your recompense in full, forevermore."

He had paid... with his life, she realized. Her face shot to the cauldron before which Briar stood. It was over. It was paid. This annum's recompense was a fallacy, if ever there was a time it had not been.

"It is finished!" Jaela cried to Briar's back. *"It is finished! It has already been paid! We are exonerated, freely and forevermore!"*

Briar twirled on her heel, eyes fixed on Jaela.

Jaela blinked back at her before her gaze drifted to the faces of those around her. By their expressions, she recognized they had understood her.

Words surged from her mouth, "The Creator sent his son to carry our iniquities and maladies into death so we would be liberated... forever. He paid our recompense with his *life*. This is why daemonkind celebrate. They believe they have won a great victory." She flung her head back in laughter. "But *we* have won. There is no longer a recompense to be paid, nor can it be. It is *finished.*"

A familiar rumbling started through the chamber.

"That is *enough*, firetongue!" the dark one thundered from the landing. "Forsake this now and I will make you my princess—ruler of the tribes! It is what I have intended for you since I discovered what you are. Cease this episode and I will receive you as my finest child. We may rule them together, you and I! You have *no concept* of what we might accomplish together!"

If Jaela had been tempted in any way, it was too late. Like the rays of the sun itself, radiance flashed from the entrance of the chamber. A man stood in silhouette. As Jaela squinted to see beyond the light, she glimpsed a body marred beyond recognition. Though he was cloaked in blood, she distinguished him by the gleaming puncture wounds in his hands.

"It is him..." she gasped in astonishment, her pulse quickening like a rapid drumbeat.

His eyes, spellbinding and amorous, flashed to her for the space of a nod before returning to the platform.

Jaela could not breathe. He was *here*, in the land of the dead. But of course this was where he would be now he was deceased. The crowd of young people fell back with unreserved perplexity as he strode through their number. With single purpose, he started up the staircase. Every step sent tremors through the expanse.

"No..." the dark one murmured with uncertainty. He fell back a step with each footfall the son made in approach. "No, *stop this*. What do you think you are doing? You have lost! What can you hope to accomplish *now?!"*

The Anointed One strode across the dais, halting before the fuming cauldron still hot with the last offering. Stretching out his hand over it, he paused to gaze into the eyes of the dark one—the one who had called himself *God*.

"N-no, you are *mine!*" the dark one bellowed. "You must do as *I* command now! *Death and the Grave,* where are you? Put this prisoner in his place!"

"It... *is*... finished..." echoed deliberately through the hall from the very lips of the son himself, more musical even than the arresting melody the dark one had composed only moments before. With the squeezing of his fist, three drops of blood dripped from his lesion into the cauldron.

For a single, magnificent moment, all was stagnant. In the next, an explosion provoked chaos. The force of the blast stirred up a mighty windstorm as the walls began to crumble. From under Rowan's shielding form, Jaela peered up at the platform to find everything gone—the cauldron, the dark one, the son of the Great One... as well as Farrow and Briar.

"Where is Briar?" she gasped above the confusion.

Rowan pried himself from his protective stance even as the walls and ceiling continued to collapse. Franticly, he searched the platform. Taking Jaela by the hand, he battled the bedlam to gain the other side of the room. They gasped in unison when they spotted her fallen form. Farrow lay beside her, pinioned by a boulder.

Jaela rushed to Briar's side while Rowan ran to the boulder. With all his might, he heaved to no avail. Elaine appeared to aid him. It would not budge. Discovering Briar's breathing was steady, Jaela leaped to help but added little strength.

With a bloodcurdling cry, Farrow returned to consciousness. Taking in the situation, his eyes met Jaela's. They beckoned her. She knelt beside him.

"That man paid my recompense?" he asked in a timorous whisper.

She nodded, taking his hand into her own.

"I am safe?" he questioned like a small boy.

She nodded again, tears dropping from her chin onto his face. *"How?"*

"He died... so you can live forever with him in Paradise," she answered, though she knew it was not her. It was HS inside her. She felt him hot in her blood. "Do you believe it, Farrow?"

His eyes glistened as he replied, "I do not know *why* he would do it, but... I saw what he did to the cauldron. I... *believe.*"

Not many more moments passed before he was gone. Jaela stood upright, batting the tears from her face. The final assurance of his eyes remained with her. She could not fully fathom what had just transpired, nor what was happening in the span of everything that lived and died, but she understood nothing was the same.

And Farrow was *safe.*

"We have to go!" Rowan called as he stooped to lift his sister's unconscious form.

The four raced from the room through the doorway that the dark one had claimed would return them safely home. When they stepped through, a number of tunnels presented themselves for selection, many of which were caved in. Rowan growled as he spun about for some clue as to their exit. Finally, his eyes fixed on Jaela.

"What do we do?"

She blinked, unaccustomed as she was to being looked to as a leader. An impulse directed her to the furthest path. She started that way, the others following without question. She shielded her face as debris descended. The Nethers quaked in protest to what was ensuing now the son had arrived. What Jaela wouldn't give to be a fly on the wall for the remainder of the proceedings. But she discovered herself far from a fly when she was summarily seized by a horde of daemons who met them on the path.

"*You!*" the largest sniveled. "This is *your* fault!" His gesture went to the disintegrating ramparts.

Despite her terror, Jaela nearly laughed. She had very little at all to do with it. She had merely stopped Briar from selling her soul to the devil. The Anointed One was the cause of all else.

"Well, lucky for you," the daemon continued grudgingly, "Luciferas has plans for you. *Come along!*"

Jaela's feet would not budge. Heat like a fire held them in place. The daemon's eyes widened to meet her gaze. With a smirk, she opened her mouth and let loose her tongue. The horde became a pile of ashes—like a dead and forgotten bonfire at evening meal. She stepped over them, casting a glance back to make certain the others were safe to follow. Though Rowan said nothing, his gaze met hers with amused wonder. Elaine was not so speechless.

"Mayhap she *is* an angel of the river people," she remarked.

Jaela shook her head. Only weeks before, she had been rumored to possess the blood of daemonkind. She had been a
"wild thing" at best. Now, she was called an angel. Well, she
was neither. She sensed the fire of the Creator's spirit sweltering
within. She was not alone—never had been, never would be. She
was a firetongue. Her life was only just beginning. That was,
if she survived the next daemonic band that approached with
swords and batons.

"You think you can escape our grasp within our own realm,
firetongue?!" a daemon with two heads roared with both
mouths from down the tunnel. "I am *Death and the Grave*. You
are treading on *my* domain. I swear upon the keys to my kingdom that you will not escape here without first surrendering
your will to my master, Luciferas!" With an animalistic roar, he
sauntered toward her as his hordes raced on around him.

Jaela's tongues sent a deluge before her, but Elaine's cry diverted her attention. She and Rowan were under attack from
behind, with poor Briar's body lying between them and her.
Voicing unintelligible speech that way, her fire passed safely
through her friends to grasp the horde beyond. Though they
squealed, only a few vanished into ash.

Next thing Jaela knew, her wrist was arrested, but the attacker
soon fell. Assailant after assailant was branded by her tongue.
Many if not most became cinders on the wind. Yet, it was clear
these were another breed of dark warriors, not so easy to assail
as those she had faced before.

Each time she earned herself a moment's freedom, she turned back to aid those behind her. It all became too much when she spotted Rowan lying unconscious beside his sister. With a yelp, she flew to his side. He breathed, but his skin was pale. She stroked his face, unconsciously casting her other hand toward the next wave of daemons to send them flying back.

"Rowan, wake up!" she cried, tears flooding her eyes. "Please, you *have* to be well."

With ferocity, she was wrenched from his side and made to face none other than Death and the Grave. His hot breath scorched her face as he snickered over her. "Not so big and bad, are you, wild thing?"

She blinked back at him. He had thought her big and bad?

All at once, his claw was prying through her lips and then her teeth. She tossed her head this way and that, but his hand soon fumbled down her throat as if he would tear out her tongue from its source. Panic nearly sent her into a faint when her blood seethed furiously. HS emerged to possess her tongue. It clicked irrepressibly, compelling the claw from her throat. Death and the Grave released Jaela to the floor, but she leaped atop him, pressing her knee into his gut as the maelstrom of her language besieged him.

"By the blood of him who gave his life!" she heard herself declare as a foreign object shot from her mouth. A sword, crimson as the blood of the son itself, landed in the hand of one she had not realized was standing by—a towering man in gleaming armor with hair and wings tossed by the winds that yet blustered from the explosion. He was not the Anointed One, as she had at first hoped. But when the weapon born of her words landed in his grasp, he demanded Death and the Grave rise to his feet.

Jaela fell back as the daemon stood to face this new assailant, drawing a black sword from somewhere at his side. The commencing warfare produced unusual effect on the plane about them. Light and darkness flashed as lightning and smoke emerged from their blades.

Upon another cry from Elaine, Jaela raced to defend her from the grasp of two daemons. The girl dropped upon the ground as they became ash. Jaela offered a hand to help Elaine to her feet. They froze as an unanticipated exchange of flame passed between their arms.

Jaela released her grasp, wondering what it could have meant. When the next line of attackers assailed them, it became all too clear. Both women breathed victorious flame against them. Jaela could not begin to grasp how or why Elaine was acting as a Firetongue, but she was spared no time for contemplation. For what felt like an age, the two defended the brother and sister laid out upon the floor. Then, at long last, they turned to find that even Death and the Grave had fled. Only the man in armor remained.

"Thanks for this," he spoke to Jaela with a wave of the crimson sword. "My previous one was badly damaged."

She blinked back at him, uncertain as to what it all denoted. Before she had time to answer, he strode past her, plucking up

Rowan and Briar under each arm. With a nod, he directed, "Follow me."

Jaela and Elaine exchanged glances before racing after the one who had carried off their comrades. It was not soothing that he seemed to know his way around, but it wasn't long before they were standing in the very place from which they had first entered the Nethers. Without warning, he tossed first Briar and then Rowan into the light that glowed above. Despite Elaine's squeal of uncertainty, he took hold of her and did the same. Finally, he approached Jaela with hands on his hips.

"They are safe," he informed. "They are within the cavern from which you came, upon the planet Kaern."

"Who *are* you?" she questioned in wonderment.

"I am Viijelyk, High Warrior of the Great One and his son, the Anointed One. They sent me to see you to safety. You have trusted them with all your heart, soul, mind and strength. They cannot and will not forsake that. Their eyes are upon you."

"I thank you," she answered with a relieved sigh, "for everything."

"I was not alone," he returned with a nod. "Despite appearances, you were well defended. And you did not do so bad yourself back there. Without your tongues to first summon and then arm me, I might never have arrived in time to help."

"Is Death and the Grave... gone forever?" she inquired hopefully.

"Nay. But he is no longer ruler of this realm. His keys have... been misplaced, shall we say?"

She shook her head in wonder and confusion, especially as she recalled the daemon's threat concerning the keys in question. "Things will never be the same, will they?"

The warrior quirked his head to the side. "Would you wish them to be?"

With a growing grin, she shook her head.

"Very well then." He stooped to lift her. "You have much to do on the other side of this portal, firetongue."

With a toss as gentle as the rocking of a babe, she flew upward, landing easily beside Elaine, who was kneeling over the siblings.

"Are they well?" Jaela asked, crouching beside Rowan to run a familiar thumb across his brow.

Elaine shook her head, revealing she understood Jaela's words. With a smirk, she added, "But they soon will be." When next her mouth opened over Briar, it was with an unusual language. Jaela bent to offer the same aid to Rowan.

CHAPTER 22

ROWAN'S EYES FLEW OPEN to the person he most wished to see. A wave of affection made his heart throb at sight of her. It was all he could do not to reach up and brush her dangling locks behind her ear. Perhaps it was a small gesture, but he feared she would read his sentiments and reject them.

Something had happened to him. Yes, he had felt himself change over the course of the journey, especially as concerned Jaela. But those alterations had come softly. After setting eyes upon the son of the Great One and witnessing what he had done for them, he felt himself an entirely new human. He was *free*. And he wasn't afraid anymore—not that he had ever admitted to being so before. Most importantly, his heart seemed to have been unlocked to tenderness he had never known before. This new liberty, he was certain, was what made him fairly dizzy with relief to find Jaela safe beside him. If he did not know any better, he might wager he was falling for his wife.

"Celestial day, firetongue," he said with a grin. Drawing himself up to a sitting position, he scanned her. "You are well?"

She nodded, eyes dropping to her hands as a smile played on her face. "As are you?"

He nodded as well, pondering her for some moments. Did she feel anything like he did? When she neglected to meet his gaze again, he tore his eyes from her long enough to see that Briar was with them. In that sweep, he ascertained their surroundings. "We are back on Kaern?" he asked incredulously.

"We are," Jaela replied.

"How did you manage it?"

She grinned largely, at last giving him her eyes. *"I* did not. It is a long story."

"And one that can be shared later," Elaine said swiftly, helping Briar to her feet. "I want out of this spooky old mountain."

Rowan sat staring back at Elaine in astonishment. Flames had exuded from her lips. It was a moment before she seemed to notice his reaction.

With the flicker of a shared glance with Jaela, she nodded. "She said it was a long story."

"Wait, what is going on?" Briar questioned. "You are like Jaela now... only I can understand you."

Elaine nodded. "Jaela helped me up and... something happened." She released an almost apprehensive gasp at the memory of it, sending her flames aflutter. "I am glad I still seem able to speak plainly. I do not have a Rowan, you know. Speaking of, you never said you could understand her during our time together, Ro...?"

Rowan blushed, chin dropping to his chest.

"It was a recent development," Briar answered, covering for him without necessarily speaking falsely. "But I am with you, Elaine. Let us be out of here. We can discuss things more comfortably in the open air."

Rowan leaped to his feet, casting a tentative glance at Jaela. He offered a hand to help her up. She accepted with a timid smile. It was a good sign. She did not hate him. That was a start.

It was nightfall when they emerged from the mountain. Though their packs had been lost in the aftermath of the Anointed One's triumph, they had reappeared in the cavern with them. They indulged in a feast prepared by Rowan and Jaela while Briar and Elaine recounted the astonishing event. It was relived with enthusiasm until it came time to explain Farrow's absence to Briar.

"But he is safe," Jaela murmured. "He believed."

Rowan translated her words for Briar's sake.

"I do not understand," Briar began, looking to Jaela. "I understood your speech in the Nethers. Why am I unable to now?"

Jaela shook her head, looking to Rowan. "I suppose... it was an impulse—an ability bestowed in the moment."

"Perhaps with practice," Elaine began, "you will be able to speak as clearly as me. It does not seem fair that I should be able to when you cannot."

Jaela nodded meditatively.

"I wonder if that is it," Briar agreed with eagerness. "I wager that, because your strange words frightened you as a child, Jaela, you stopped speaking so long that you lost the knack for our people's language. Perhaps as you and Rowan speak together, the tongue of the tribes will return."

Despite how different he felt, Rowan's remorse concerning his secret persisted. What if Briar was right? What if practice was all Jaela had required in order to speak correctly? He had not realized his regret was so apparent until Jaela's hand rested on his.

"It is behind us now," she said with uncharacteristic sternness. "I forgive you. Let us... be friends?"

Scarcely without thinking, Rowan flipped his hand over to grasp hers in his own before releasing it. There was a message in his handclasp that he both hoped and dreaded she might read.

~>>>>>> <<<<<~

Jaela awoke to the piquant fragrance of Old Willow's fiery roses. She questioned when they had arrived in Blooms before her eyes opened to reveal a forest glowing in the morning light. They were still beside the mountain that contained a gateway to the Nethers. The thought made her shiver. Yet, she arose with a smile as she followed the beckoning perfume. Bobbing rosebushes hailed her into her hollow tree.

"Celestial sunrise, Jaela," HS greeted pleasantly.

"Celestial sunrise," she replied with a smile. "Do you realize you have completely changed my world by sending me on this journey?"

With a chuckle, he answered, "Do you realize it was my purpose? Or part of it. There is more to be done."

"Did I not do what I was meant back in the Nethers?"

"That was a start. Now, I need you to do it over and over again."

"Do *what* exactly?" she asked with a brow raised.

"Tell the world what you told the champions. Fill others with my essence like you did Elaine. Destroy the powers of darkness. Come into agreement with my angelic warriors for the sake of my peoples. You see... it is not much. Just this one little thing."

Jaela laughed freely. "But *how* will I tell people? They will not understand me."

"I suppose you will work it out."

She narrowed her eyes. "You let me march into an awfully hopeless situation, you know. When last we spoke like this, you knew I was on the path to the Forbidden Pass. You knew what lay before me. Why did you not *stop* me?"

"Stop you?" he asked incredulously. "That was my birthday gift to you."

Further words were choked from her throat as her eyes flashed back and forth between his. Finally, she stammered, "*HS,* you cannot be serious! Y-you... you wanted me to... be ensnared in marriage to-to *him?*" She felt her face flush deeply.

"Why do you think I pressed you to forgive him? It would have made the whole affair much more pleasant."

"Pleasant?!" she cried, leaping to her feet. "We are trapped! And you *wanted* this?"

He chuckled, settling her beside himself as he draped an arm about her shoulders. "I wish only the very best for you. Perhaps you will see this in time. For now, do you agree to the remainder of my request? Will you go for me? Not only to each and every tribe but to the continents of this world, imparting what you have learned?

"Before you answer, I must warn you that your message will not always, or even often, be accepted. You will be rejected and even feel yourself in great peril at times. But as you know, I am always with you. You are never alone."

Jaela considered his words carefully. She did not hesitate in her reply. "Of course I will go." Her breath was nearly taken by how much easier it was to agree to his request than it had been before she had departed from Deerskin. Had she truly changed so much in so short a time? The Great One certainly worked in mystifying ways.

With the squeezing of her form against his, he rubbed her arm. "That is my girl, my firetongue. But please make clear to them that what is offered, and accepted or rejected, is not just salvation from the Nethers. It is a way of life. We extend a whole new reality—a kingdom that must be all or nothing. This proposal cannot be accepted by halves but wholes or they may be spit out. Show them the miracles, teach them the way and make them an offer that cannot be refused."

"Indeed," she answered, "who could refuse it?"

"You would be surprised," he answered wistfully.

She tilted her head back to peer into his face. "What is it?"

"It is only that... we love them so. We will always love them. That never ends... *ever.*"

"And that is... a problem?"

With a sigh, he peered down to say, "It *is* when they rebuff the Anointed One. Now that he has departed from the Nethers, we shall not enter there again. Those who do not embrace him choose eternity without us. It... is a tragic affair."

She sat up from his chest. *"He has left the Nethers?"*

The broken cloud in his eyes gave way to cheery flame. "He *has*. By my watch..." To her bewilderment, he checked his wrist. "He has just appeared alive again before a very dear lady. She is the first to share the news of his return... That is no small potatoes, Jaela."

"HS... *how?* He is—was—dead."

"He is *not*. Death and the Grave could not hold him. The Anointed One now holds those keys. So, he brought himself back to life."

"He holds the keys..." she murmured in bemused amazement. "And he revived himself... Surely, he is the son of God."

"Surely," he answered with like wonder. "And you will explain this to the clans along your journey home?"

"I can go home? I thought—"

"You must see your mother first. You must tell her everything—"

"Of course!" she interrupted with delight. "Oh, of *course.*" She threw her arms about his neck in an embrace. "Thank you, HS. She will be thrilled!"

As HS had bidden, Jaela and her party stopped at every village they passed along the route to Deerskin. Without batting an eye,

Rowan stepped into the position of translating for Jaela. He seemed to enjoy repeating her words with fervor and excitement. Most of the time, the people could not help but respond to his charisma as well as HS's power presented by Jaela and Elaine. At other times, their telling fell upon deaf ears. From these places, they were driven from the vicinity.

"It is as if they *like* sending their young to pay the recompense every annum," Briar muttered irritably as she pried a pebble from her cheek. "And who throws *stones* at strangers anymore?"

"They do not understand what is required of the champions," Elaine acknowledged.

"But they know it means grave danger!"

The group fell silent. Yet, they persisted in this new mission for the remainder of the journey home. Jaela was amazed at what occurred when the son's sacrifice was embraced. Sometimes it was only part of a village who believed. Other times it was merely one or two. But by the time they reached the Tribe of Blooms, the news was traveling like wildfire. It could not be contained. Sometimes, the tribes expected them even before their arrival, having heard rumors of what they could do and the irregular news they carried from their exploit into the Nethers.

The day they arrived in Blooms, Old Willow was the first to welcome them. She stepped from a row of shrubberies to throw her arms around Jaela.

"Ya restored my years!" she cried. "What a time I had explainin' it to the others. But now we've been hearin' *tales* of you all, includin' you, Miss Elaine." She patted the girl's cheek before returning her attention to Jaela. "Didn't I tell ya we'd be hearin' about ya? Now, everyone is expectin' *quite* a demonstration. There's young Ladd, who has lost the use of a leg. I told 'em ya could mend him. We've even got folks from other villages awaitin' yer arrival." She stole an arm around Jaela to usher her into the village.

The first set of eyes to spot them was Jethro's. Jaela had all but forgotten he existed until he came racing to meet them. "You have returned!" he cried with eyes merrily searching the group. "Where is Farrow? Farrow!" he called beyond, as if his brother was loitering.

Elaine grasped his arms, peering steadily into his eyes. "I need to tell you a story about a man called the Anointed One."

"What is wrong with your voice?" he questioned. "You are like that comely girl—I-I mean Jaela of Deerskin." His eyes refused to meet Jaela's under his blush.

Elaine shook her head with gravity. "Did you hear me, Jethro?"

His face dropped. "Er... yes. Wh-why?"

"Because we entrusted your brother to him."

His brows rose as he allowed Elaine to escort him into the village. When a number of children spotted them, they went about shouting, "The fire-angel is here!" Jaela blushed at the nickname. Little did they know they now possessed their own firetongue. This tribe would be richly favored if they chose to accept Elaine for what she now was. Before she knew it, a crowd had gathered, shouting salutations and questioning Farrow's absence. She felt for them. It was clear he had been a beloved member of the community. And he was supposed to have been their champion. But the champions had been eclipsed by someone so much greater. Farrow had reaped the benefit of it.

The crowd fell silent as they parted for a child who was laid at Jaela's feet.

"This is my boy, Ladd," spoke a man she presumed to be the father. "Can you help him, fire-angel?"

Jaela deliberated some moments before stepping aside and pressing Elaine to the forefront. "These are your people," she reminded her. "The testimony will mean more coming from you."

With a comradely grin, Elaine knelt before the boy. "Hey, Laddie. Heard you hurt yourself."

He nodded, eyes beaming at the surprise of finding that a girl from his own tribe shared Jaela's fire.

Without further ado, Elaine put her hand to his leg. "All right, Laddie-boy. You can get up."

His eyes shot to the leg. "You mean...?"

She nodded, pursing her lips together with scarcely contained delight. "Come on, fella," she urged. "Hop up!"

With a glowing grin, he did just that. The crowd gasped and cheered, looking to their stand-in champion with awe and bewilderment. Elaine lost no time in explaining.

"This is not my power you have witnessed, nor even Jaela's. What we share is a gift from the Creator." It was clear she would have gone on when a line formed before her.

"I told you you'd be busy," Old Willow reminded with a grin.

For the remainder of the afternoon, they restored the wounded and infirm. At the end of the line awaited a surprise even for them. Jaela's face shone with compassion when she knelt before the cold, still form a little girl.

"Hespa!" Elaine gasped, kneeling beside the body. Her eyes flew to the parents. "What happened?"

"She took ill..." the mother sobbed. "Can you... do something?"

Elaine turned to Jaela with little hope, but Jaela's eyes reminded her of what they already knew. The Anointed One was so powerful that he had raised his own body from the dead. Due to HS, this was the power they wielded. There was a possibility.

"Tell them his story," Jaela directed as she studied Hespa's frame.

Tremulously, Elaine returned to her feet. "Many of you have asked where Farrow may be found. I will tell you. As he put it in his own words, he is *safe*. That is what he stated in the moments he lay dying for the sake of his village."

Moans sounded as a woman's sob was heard.

"Farrow witnessed what few did," Elaine continued. "He watched the son of the Creator pay the recompense for the tribes—for *mankind*—forevermore. Because Farrow saw, he believed. But there will be many who believe without seeing because their heart tells them it is true. Because of this hope, Farrow is safe within the realm of the Creator. His salvation was paid in full by the Anointed One.

"Friends and family," she continued with an emotional hiccup, "the recompense need never be paid again. There need be no more quests into the Nethers and no more sacrifices made for our salvation. We are saved. Do you believe it?"

"Yes," sounded from the ground.

All eyes shot to where Hespa lay, staring up with wide eyes into Elaine's face. "I believe it. I saw Farrow myself." She sat up, sending gasps and shrieks through her people. "I saw Farrow with the Creator. He was *delighted*. I wished to stay, but it seems it was not my time. Mama needs me too much."

That supposition was answered as the wailing mother, followed by the father, fell upon the daughter. "It is all right, Mumsy," Hespa soothed. "I am well. And so is Farrow."

Jaela's gaze flew to the woman she surmised to be Farrow's mother. She was held tightly within Jethro's arms. Her tear-filled eyes glowed as she gazed down at Hespa in her parent's embrace. Then, she looked to Jaela.

"He is well?" she asked.

Jaela nodded, echoes of Farrow's own assurance replaying in her mind's eye.

With a relieved sob, the mother turned her face into her son's chest.

CHAPTER 23

THE FOLLOWING DAY, JAELA sped through her grooming and breakfasting, scarcely sparing a moment to greet anyone. Her mind was set upon one thing—what she had desired most since the day she had left her village behind.

"Are you well?" Rowan asked when she bumped into him on her way to retrieve her pack.

With a blush, she stepped back. "I am. I go to see my mother today."

"Aaah," he replied with understanding. "Did you intend to leave us behind?"

"If I had to," she admitted. "I cannot wait any longer. I could scarcely catch a wink last night. She is so near."

"Well, allow me to fetch my pack. Briar will wish to come, too."

"Are you leaving us so soon?" Elaine questioned when she entered their dwelling unannounced. "But we have so much work to do."

Jaela nodded. "The work is yours, Elaine."

Elaine considered her some moments before, "I am not sure I know what I am doing."

"You are filled with the spirit-essence of the Great One. Seek him with your whole heart and he will instruct you."

Elaine nodded. "I cannot seem to bear parting from you all. Everything is so different from when we left here together."

Briar threw an arm about Elaine. "We live a day away, lady. This is not the last of us. We will be back."

The three scarcely managed to escape from the Tribe of Blooms. Though the village had Elaine, they were loath to release Jaela. She could not help being amused by this. They had been so uncertain of her when she had left them the first time. With her face turned to her home village, her stomach turned with questions.

"What is the matter?" Rowan probed as he lifted the pack from her back to place upon his own. "I thought you could not wait to see your mother."

"I..." She let her fire fade as she reflected. "I have grown accustomed to seeing myself differently than I used to."

He considered her some moments before, "You fear the judgements of our people will set you back?"

She heaved a sigh. "I do." Quirking a brow at him, she asked, "Am I silly?"

He shook his head. "I understand. And I am sorry again for not helping you in past. I fully intend to amend that now."

She nodded as fresh qualms arose. "Rowan... I hardly know how to approach this..."

His eyes scanned her with concern. "Yes?"

"Will you... conceal your, er, ring? And I will hide mine?"

She was not prepared for the heaviness that disturbed his whole form. It was suddenly as if he conveyed a dozen burdens. But why? Did he somehow think she would be embarrassed to be seen as his wife?

"Please do not misunderstand me," she added quickly. "We are already returning so changed. I..." How could she explain that she could not bear to witness the diminishing of their people's reverence for him when they learned he was wedded to the wild thing? She did not have the words.

Neither did Rowan speak as he removed his ring. When he held out his hand, she surmised he would take hers, too. She was surprised by how much it troubled her to remove it. She had not realized how accustomed she had become to it sitting upon her finger, nor how often she had unconsciously daydreamed over it. What would he do with them now? Her heart ached as he stuffed them into his pocket like a satchel of hazelnuts.

Not having seemed to notice the exchange, Briar sounded off on how thrilled she was to see their parents again. Jaela was grateful for this sister-in-law, who was so gifted with filling silences. She could not help feeling ill over Rowan's reaction. She was suddenly struck by the likelihood of his simply not liking to be reminded of their union. Had she expected him to make her keep the ring as he went shouting their nuptials from the rooftops of Deerskin?

Rowan's parents greeted him with swift embrace. Briar was similarly received, though with some rebukes for the way she had left. The parents seated their children in order to gather details of their heroism. The arguments that followed the telling proved the siblings had no real feats of their own to speak of. Their parents certainly did not wish to hear about Jaela's triumphs. They would not even entertain the notion of the Creator having a son. In the end, they determined their children had failed to save the tribes.

"Father," Rowan pleaded, "I understand you sacrificed yourself to save Deerskin those years ago. Perhaps you find it difficult to believe us because you feel you have already sold your soul to the dark one… But the life of the Anointed One is worth more than enough to purchase—"

With enraged eyes, Bowan cut his son off with a swift rebuke. "That is never to be spoken of again!"

When his father's eyes flew to his wife, Rowan realized that not even his mother understood the state of affairs. Rowan had nearly forgotten it was meant to be a secret. He was simply unable to comprehend the fact that his was an ancestry of champions who had surrendered themselves to a dark one with a god complex. He would have been one of them. But the Anointed One, with Jaela's aid, had spared him. That was no small matter. He was *safe*… and he was no longer the person he used to be.

He vacated the house. Briar could press the matter if it pleased her. But having lost the pride of their parents was going to make things difficult. Perhaps that was best. Pride had been his downfall for too many years.

As he ambled through the forest with hands in his pockets, he recalled how often Jaela had spoken of telling her mother of the testimony they had woven throughout the tribes. Her one thought had been to practice the tale in order to perfect it for Evangeline's hearing. As a woman who had lost her ability to be cleansed because of the loss of the River Lifespring, he could only imagine what it would mean to her. It now occurred to him that it must be difficult for Jaela to convey. Would it be presumptuous for him to turn up at their door? He started that way, but turned back to the forest. Pausing for some moments, he finally continued toward their home again.

Jaela answered the door with a grin that froze at the sight of him. *"Rowan? Do you need something?"*

Evangeline arrived behind her. "Rowan?" she questioned in her turn. "My daughter speaks freely to you?" In astonishment, she looked from him to Jaela and back again.

He nodded, unable to remove his eyes from Jaela's face. They had only been apart for a short time and already he had missed her. That was certainly telling and it did not bode well for him. "I can translate her words," he explained to the mother. "It is why I came. May I... help you communicate?"

Jaela fairly yanked him into the room by his shirt sleeve. "I have been trying for ages, but it is far too much to explain through gestures." She proceeded to press him into a chair before the fire, patting the pillow behind him to make certain he was comfortable.

Rowan was astonished by this welcome. His eyes wandered about the delightfully adorned room. It was a pleasant place that told stories as to the years of intimate friendship between the mother and daughter. He felt he was gaining new insights into Jaela and appreciated her all the more.

"Tell Mother *everything,*" she urged as she pulled up a bench in order for her and Evangeline to sit beside him. "From the beginning."

Rowan enjoyed disclosing their story to someone who responded to every turn of events with such animation. It was as if Evangeline was living it with them as she gasped and squealed with wide-eyed wonder. But as he neared revealing the episode within the Nethers, he feared the truth would produce a similar response to that of his parents.

But before he reached that juncture, he was forced to admit his ability to understand her daughter's speech. Though she was dumbfounded, she presented no rebukes, only urging him to proceed with the narration. Then, of course, came the wedding ceremony. Eluding Jaela's gaze, he opted to skip it.

With great care, he walked Evangeline through the happenings surrounding the Cauldron of Recompense. The woman became completely still. With uncertainty, he completed the tale of their escape from the Nethers, as well as the visit Jaela had received from the spirit of the Great One.

Finally, he cast his eyes to the fire, avoiding the disbelief and condemnation that must show on her face. But his gaze flew up again at the echo of Evangeline's gut-wrenching sob. Her head lay upon her daughter's shoulder as if she was the child. Rowan questioned what she had made of the tale. Did she fear the damnation of their tribe?

Jaela met his eyes with a teary smile. "She is safe."

Rowan's brows rose to his hairline. Evangeline believed. Could that mean there was hope for his parents? Or was Jaela's mother so eager to embrace it because she had been of the River's Way? Perhaps it was the bond with her daughter that made her so trusting. Before he knew it, he was upon his feet, freshly determined to convince his parents of the truth.

Evangeline stood with him, taking his hand into her soft one. "You are not *leaving?*" she questioned expressively. "I have not thanked you properly. You must remain for... for tea?" The vulnerability in her expression conveyed she did not often, if ever, entertain company.

"I would love to," he answered with ease as he retook his seat.

Jaela's satisfied grin made him hope as he had not dared as yet. He wished he was free to inform Evangeline of what she rightfully was to him. Already, he liked this lawful mother of his and felt she could like him. The problem lay with Jaela. Must they go on this way forever, living as if the lawful union had not occurred? Would Rowan spend his whole life pretending he had not fallen in love with Jaela the Firetongue?

If she would not receive his affection, he would give it in other ways. He spent half a fortnight depicting her heroic power to the people of their village. He told them of how she had saved *him*, defended *him*, protected *him*. He was not certain anyone would have believed him if it wasn't for Briar. As some began to insinuate that Jaela had cast a daemonic spell on him, Briar doggedly defended his account. At one point, she went so far as to nearly spill the beans about the marriage before he promptly elbowed her.

When later they were alone in their home, she asked, "Why are you concealing your bond with Jaela? By the way you have described her to our village, I thought you admired her. I cannot *believe* you are already falling back into your old ways."

"It is not *me*, Briar. It is Jaela. She asked me to hide the rings." He obtained the leather cord from within his tunic, revealing the rings that hung concealed over his chest.

Her eyes fell to his finger. "I *had* wondered... But why should she be ashamed? You are the finest fellow I know!"

His gaze dropped to the rings as he slipped them on and off the tip of his finger. "I do not know... I suppose she wishes to go on as if it never happened."

Briar flew to her feet. "I am going to have a talk with her."

Stuffing the cord back into hiding, he grasped her arm. "You *cannot.*"

"*Why not?*"

"If she cannot love me back, I will not have her live as if she does."

"You are *in love* with Jaela?" she asked with a dumbfounded grin.

He nodded, scarcely concealing the bliss over the way his heart throbbed with what he suffered for the firetongue. Perhaps he felt this way because it was so novel or perhaps he would always feel thus. Either way, he could not abide the thought of being separated from her. She may insist upon it if he pressed his suit. If mere friendship was all he could attain, it must be enough.

"What is this about Jaela?" their mother probed as she entered the room with stunned expression. "Rowan, this is *unacceptable*. I understand you two have convinced the village that girl is some kind of hero, but I still recall when she was rumored to possess daemon blood. I hope you realize we expect better for you. Caspa has planned practically everything concerning your nuptials. You have not *spoken* to the wild little thing, have you?"

Rowan thrust his hands into his pockets as he turned to gaze out the window. He had no way of knowing how much his mother had heard, nor was he certain how much he wished her to know. For so long, he had worked to conceal his defects and struggles because he knew they, too, would be considered unacceptable. His parents could not conceive of how to offer guidance. And since they believed their children had been hood-winked into forsaking the recompense, they were on the brink of casting them out of the home. What wouldn't they do if they learned Rowan was married to the "wild little thing?" He knew he could more than take care of himself if cast out, but he did not wish to leave that way. He loved his parents. He wanted them to be *safe*.

"Have you not *seen* what Jaela can do?" Briar questioned their mother. "She has been performing *miracles*—healing the sick, even *bringing people back to life*. Is that not enough for you for a lawful daughter?"

"Lawful daughter...?" the mother gasped. *"Nethers forbid.* Rowan, will you look at me? I require an oath that you will not so much as *think* about making that vile forest sprite such a thing to me. *Rowan?"*

Mutely, Rowan passed through the room and sauntered out of the house. If things went as he hoped, he might never enter it again. He directed his feet toward Jaela's home. It was where he had spent most of his time since their return. Jaela and Evangeline markedly enjoyed his company. After all, they struggled to communicate effectively without him. But even beyond that, time flew when they were together. He knew it was their understanding concerning the Anointed One that made the difference.

"Rowan!" Evangeline greeted merrily after his rap upon the door. "You are about in time for noon meal. You will join us?"

"I would be *pleased* to," he replied. Turning to Jaela, he spoke with somberness, "May we speak privately first?"

Jaela's brows rose with a blend of surprise and anxiety before she led him out the door. Waving a swift hand to her mother, she closed it behind them. Neither spoke a word as they strolled into the solitude of the forest. At long last, she sat down upon a fallen tree, patting the place beside her. "What is it, Rowan?"

His eyes surveyed how she sat bidding him to sit with her. Would she welcome him any further into her life? Taking the proffered seat, he spared no time in turning to her with, "I hear you will soon be leaving."

She blinked back it him. "How can you know?"

"Briar."

She nodded, pursing her lips. It was evident she had not bidden Briar to share the decision. "Well, yes..." she replied, "I must go. I promised HS, you know, that I would... well, that I would tell the whole world about the recompense. I have not informed half the tribes as yet."

"That is what I came to see you about," he began with a nod. "You see... you need me. You know you do. They are not likely to appreciate your speeches without me."

When she opened her mouth to speak, he rushed on, "I want you to know how different I feel after everything. The quest itself altered me. But my whole heart and mind are transformed after seeing the son of the Great One. I was so *lost* before, so taken up with attempting perfection... or at least appearing so. I do not carry that anymore.

"But I want you to know how much more capable of love I feel myself to be. And... my heart seems to be filled with a particular person whom I so happen to be fortunate enough to call my wife, at least in my heart."

Once again, her lips parted to respond, but he was not yet finished. "Jaela, I do not ask you to accept what happened between us at the Clan of Covenants. I only ask to join you in your travels. I promise I can make myself useful, not only translating but defending. I can keep guard and make certain you take care of yourself... or even do it for you if you cannot"

His speech was cut short by the seizing of his hands by hers. Her eyes surveyed him with gentleness some moments before, "I love you, Rowan of Deerskin."

The fire that drifted into Rowan's face warmed him with relief such as he had never had cause to feel in his life. *"Thank the Great One,"* he breathed.

AFTERWORD

A Legend of Jaela the Firetongue or
The Birth of the Greater Archipelagos
as told by Chamaeleo the Shifter in the book
Seeker's Revolution: Book Three of the Seeker's Trilogy

Jaela's tale originated long before the kingdom of Kierelia of the planet Kaern was yet dreamed of, when the tribes of its southern region were ungoverned. Jaela's heart was very near the Great One's and his to hers. She was his dearest friend upon the plane, as she had vowed every piece of herself to him. Still, after her many years of service for his unearthly kingdom, he desired to give her more. He gazed long upon the stars to consider a gift.

One day, he led Jaela and her husband, Rowan, to the cavern of a looming mountain, revealing that he had conceived an exceptional surprise. Jaela peered up into the Great One's face with an adoring smile, pondering his intentions. She knew from prior experience they would be nothing short of just who he was and he was *marvelous*. Turning to her husband, she raised a daring brow and stepped into the cavern.

They had no torch with which to see but for the Great One's sheer glory as it trailed behind. Jaela attempted to touch the shimmering splendor with her fingers, but it fluttered and danced around her, into her fingertips and through her hair.

When they reached the conclusion of the cavern's passage, there resided a radiant, shifting veil. The sight of it might have alarmed another couple, but in all their travels over the face of Kaern, they had seen much. With an intrigued smirk, Jaela stepped through the portal and into a vast desert land.

As the couple surveyed their new surroundings, the Great One's voice emanated from the skies above with bubbling joy as he announced, "This land is yours, Jaela. I fashioned it for you. It is all *yours.*"

Her mouth opened in wonder. She understood it was a new world and, though it was plain, it was *hers*. Dropping to her knees, she sobbed out, "How *great* is your love for me?"

The moment her first tear dropped upon the sandy plain, a magnificent substance shot forth, cloaking the land with a vast sea of bluest water. Jaela and Rowan laughed with incredulity as they swam in the deep that now covered the world.

The Great One spoke momentously, "As wide and deep and great and *vast* as this ocean, that is my love for you."

He proceeded to lay his fingers to various regions of water from which beautifully flourishing islands were breathed into existence. They bloomed expressively with flowers, trees and mountains, as well as creatures that roared, buzzed, crawled and flew.

As Jaela witnessed the spectacle, she sank beneath the ocean's surface in wonder of it all. But the Great One shed his glory upon her once again and raised her from the sea, saying, "This is my love for you, dearest one. *This* is my love for you."

He gently placed the couple upon the soft sand of the nearest archipelago and stretched out beside them with head rested upon his bent-up arm.

"How do you like it?" he asked with eagerness.

Jaela released a great laugh despite her tear-filled eyes. "I think it will do," she murmured with bursting pleasure.

The three discoursed until a young sun set upon the new land and the uniquely designed stars and galaxies unveiled themselves above.

DEAR READER,

You MADE IT TO the end... and I rather hope you enjoyed it! If you have questions regarding this tale, especially as concerns the Anointed One, do not hesitate to reach out through my website.

If you sense the tug of the Great One to accept the free gift of His Son, it is simply done. Talk to Him. Confess to an imperfect nature in need of the one and only Savior, Jesus. Vocalize your desire to follow His example. Surrender to His purposes for your life. Read His Word, The Holy Bible, and speak to Him daily.

This creed, when uninhibited by compromise, can lead to adventurous and rewarding paths. For, the God Who made the world and died for it moves in ways both mysterious and kindhearted. He desires to prosper you and not to harm you, to give you a hope-filled future. Remember, He can do anything. Nothing is too difficult for Him and nothing impossible.

With love,
Cassandra Boyson

OTHER BOOKS BY CASSANDRA BOYSON...

ABOUT THE AUTHOR

Cassandra Boyson is older than she looks but younger than the sum of her years dictates. Based out of the Dallas, Texas area, she is author of Amazon bestselling Christian Fantasy series, *The Seeker's Trilogy*. Her books focus on inspiring the supernatural walk every Christian is destined to live out as Jesus did, as well as the only means of salvation and the matchless, intimate friendship of the Great One.

CassandraBoyson.com